Final Operation

Elaine L. Orr

Copyright © 2019 Elaine L. Orr
All rights reserved.
ISBN- 978-1-0882-8637-1
Library of Congress Control Number: 2019907335

FINAL OPERATION

ELAINE L. ORR

BOOK 3 OF THE LOGLAND MYSTERY SERIES

Final Operation is a work of fiction. All characters are products of the author's imagination.

Lifelong Dreams Publishing
Copyright 2019
All rights reserved

www.elaineorr.com
www.elaineorr.blogspot.com
ISBN 13: 978-1-0882-8637-1
Library of Congress Control Number: 2019907335

Dedication

To all the small-town city and county officials who work hard every day with limited resources.
Released on my sister Diane's birthday, because she's the best.

Elaine L. Orr

Acknowledgements

Special thanks to the Decatur Critique Group (Angela, Dave, Debbie, Marilyn, and Sue), and to Karen Musser Nortman, a terrific beta reviewer.

Elaine L. Orr

CHAPTER ONE

THE BRIGHT daffodils and crocuses in the Bully Pulpit's window boxes looked peaceful, but a debate raged inside. Mayor Sharon Humphrey barely contained her temper as she addressed City Councilman Adrian Gangle. "That's ridiculous. Logland, Illinois may be a small city, but we need a police station."

Gangle leaned across the booth. "Listen Sharon, we'd save almost three quarters of a million in rent, salaries and equipment..."

"Rubbish. The line item last year was a little more than $600,000."

"Pension contributions are in another part of the budget. They're huge." Gangle sat back, a smirk on his lips.

Mayor Humphrey took the fork from her Cobb salad and gestured at Gangle. "You've been drinking Donald Dingle's Kool-Aid. You can't look at simply one side of a ledger. You have to consider the benefits."

"Madam Mayor, we've had two murders in the past year. How effective are the members of our police department?"

"You can't stop people from killing each other. What matters is that the local police took the killers off the street."

A man's shadow interrupted the two combatants. "Ma'am, sir? Maybe you don't know how loud you're talking?"

Mayor Humphrey flushed as she looked at him. "I'm sorry, Nick."

Gangle seemed unperturbed. "It'll all be out in the open at the council meeting tonight."

Marti Kerkoff came up behind Nick Hume,. though she was so short no one noticed her until she spoke. "The council meeting would be a good place to have this discussion."

Gangle looked from the two Bully Pulpit owners to the college students two booths away, and then to a family with two young children in a corner booth. All stared at him. He shrugged. "I have to get back to work." He slid out of the booth, easily reaching Nick's height of almost six feet. He handed Nick a ten-dollar bill and left through the diner's glass front door.

"Marti, Nick..." Mayor Humphrey began.

Marti waved a hand. "No worries. He was the loud one, not you."

A man about nineteen in a Sweathog Agricultural College sweatshirt laughed. "That guy puts the bully in Bully Pulpit."

WITH ALL THE TALK about abolishing the Police Department, Marti left Nick in charge of the diner that evening and went to the City Council meeting to find out what all the uproar was about. The spring air grew cold after sunset, so she wore a lightweight jacket and hid her disorganized brown hair under a brown felt beret.

The courthouse was only two blocks from the diner, and Marti walked quickly. She didn't want to stand for a long meeting.

She passed City Hall, a small building off the town square, and headed for the large county courthouse in the middle of the square. The mayor and council used one of its formal courtrooms for larger meetings, and from what Marti had heard, half the town would be there tonight.

Several people greeted her as she hurried into the courthouse. Less than a year ago, she was finishing at Illinois

Agricultural College, which Nick and his friends gleefully called Sweathog College, planning to leave Logland for good.

Bully Pulpit owner Ben's death changed everything. She and Nick would inherit the diner if they operated it for five years. She'd never imagined herself a business owner attending meetings with important people.

She hurried into the courtroom and sat next to the bookstore owner, Alice, in one of the last available seats in the wood-paneled courtroom. Alice had her long hair in a French braid, and Marti noticed her white roots. Lately, Alice had been going longer between colorings at Ramona's Ringlets Hair Salon. Marti had begun to suspect bookstore business had slowed.

She took in the room. The five-council members faced the audience from one side of a large wooden conference table. Two tables had been put together, so those who signed the list to speak sat about ten feet from the city officials, backs to the attendees.

Alice leaned toward Marti. "Did you ever see so many charts and graphs hung around a room?"

"Not since a college economics class. What are all those easels for?"

Alice lowered her voice to a whisper. "They have information about what the city spent and what the mayor wants the council to approve for next fiscal year. I think Mr. Dingle thinks all those numbers make him look smart."

"They're his charts?" Marti didn't think Dingle talented enough to do all the calculations behind the graphs.

"I suppose he thinks that if the city budget people prepare them they become his personal property," Alice murmured.

Mayor Humphrey entered from a side door near the front of the large room and took her place among the City Council members, with City Clerk Donald Dingle on her right.

"Mayor loves to make an entrance," Alice whispered. "Looks like that navy blue suit is new."

Marti nodded. As usual, the mayor's severely cut style of clothes made her look more like sixty than fifty. She contrasted with Donald Dingle's rumpled brown suit that Marti guessed he bought twenty years ago. Or maybe thirty.

The mayor tapped a gavel lightly, and Marti looked around the room. Given conversations she'd overheard in the diner the last few days, she expected to see most of the downtown business owners. She wasn't disappointed.

Gene, owner of Man-Up Tattoos, had squeezed his muscled bulk into a white dress shirt. Next to him sat the ever-nervous Squeaky Miller, whose dry cleaners and laundromat were next to the tattoo parlor, across from the diner.

Cookie shop owner Doris Minx sat next to salon owner Ramona, who hardly came to any town events. Behind the two women were Police Chief Elizabeth Friedman and Officer Tony Calderone. He was most often the person who interviewed people after a crime of any sort.

The audience rustled into silence as the mayor began to speak. "It's good to see so many residents at our annual budget hearing. To have meaningful discussions, we need input from..."

Gene called from his seat in the third row. "How soon can we tell you what we think about this bunk about getting rid of the cops?"

Muttered comments throughout the room repeated the question. Marti thought it was the college president who added, "Busy schedules. We've read the advance materials."

Marti hadn't, but didn't care to. She just knew that when anything happened in the diner, she wanted to pick up the phone and know that Tony or one of the other guys would be at the diner in two minutes.

Mayor Humphrey again tapped her gavel lightly. "First we're going to discuss additional funds for the community health center, then we'll move to law enforcement."

Marti had a hard time keeping her chin off her chest as Mr. Dingle and the city budget director discussed grants that Logland had applied for to keep the clinic afloat. From conversations in the diner, Marti knew no one opposed providing free care when someone couldn't pay. They wanted the funds to come from someplace besides the city budget. Everyone thought taxes were too high.

Final Operation

When the boring money discussion drew to a close, three people – two women who looked to be in their forties and a man about fifty – stood from various parts of the room and walked toward the mayor and council.

Mayor Humphrey consulted papers in front of her. "Yes. We have representatives of the Care Center's Client Advocacy Group."

The politicians sat straighter in their chairs and a couple of them smiled. Donald Dingle opened a large binder and flipped pages. Marti had the impression he wanted the people across from him to think he didn't care about what they would say.

When the Mayor asked the three to identify themselves, Marti learned they were Samuel Franklin, Margaret Turner, and Dorothy Washington. Everyone in town knew Mrs. Washington's name. She headed the historical society and led her family's lumber yard business. She was also the wealthiest black woman in the county.

Samuel Franklin gave an impassioned plea to be sure the health center continued a "robust staffing level." Without them, he didn't think he would have survived a heart attack long enough to be transferred to the local hospital and then air-lifted to Springfield.

Margaret Turner and Dorothy Washington had less positive comments.

Turner believed the long wait for an appointment contributed to her husband, who had diabetes, having to have his foot amputated.

Marti glanced around the room. No way to tell if anyone had a prosthetic foot. Maybe in the summer, when everyone wore shorts.

Turner picked up steam. "What you people don't realize is that small amounts of money can make a big difference at the health center. You talk about your fiscal years. You need to let the center have the money you agree to when you decide to give it. I've heard sometimes you delay and then you lose money. Some sort of matching money thing."

"Matching grant money," the mayor said. "We did lose a grant one time because the application didn't get in on time. It's regrettable."

"Regrettable to you, maybe. But could be a hundred people can't get an appointment, that's what it is. My husband, he'll never play basketball with Jordan again..." Turner stopped, put two fingers on her lips to keep from crying, and waved a hand. "I've said what I had to say. You need to put your priorities where it counts."

Dorothy Washington's voice filled the room. "I want to address my comments to Mr. Donald Dingle."

Muttering moved through the room. Dingle shut the binder he'd been leafing through, and scowled. It made him look older than his mid-seventies. Marti had heard several lunch conversations from people who wished he'd retire. Mostly city employees he'd chewed out. She couldn't figure out why anyone that old would keep working.

"Mr. Dingle," Washington's voice rose, "I want to know what the hold-up is in spending budget money to hire a pediatric nurse practitioner."

Mayor Humphrey began to respond, but Washington shook a finger in her direction. "It's Donald Dingle who said he had to delay giving the Community Health Center that money. You let him tell it."

Dingle smiled in what Marti thought was a patronizing manner.

"The Logland Community Health Center has never had a nurse practitioner," he said. "I wasn't sure all the budget numbers were practical."

"I'm well aware we haven't had one," Washington said. "Despite having needed one for many years. You told the Health Center Client Advocacy Group the city had not received the grant money expected for the position."

Humphrey raised her voice. "Grant money? Those funds were from the city's contribution to the health center budget. No grant money was involved."

Final Operation

Before Dingle could respond, Medical Examiner Skelly rose from his seat in the audience. "I also checked before this meeting. The nurse position is to come from tax-funded money. If the health center had a pediatric nurse practitioner there'd be a lot fewer ER visits."

Dingle almost snarled, "No one asked you, Dr. Hutton."

Doris Minx spoke from her seat. "He would know."

Marti added her voice to a bunch of others that said things like, "Yes he does," and "A lot better than you."

The mayor banged her gavel and looked directly at Dorothy Washington. "I will personally see that those funds are released tomorrow so the hiring process can begin."

Scattered applause turned into steady clapping. Dingle reddened, and Mayor Humphrey said, "Next we'll turn to the law enforcement budget."

The three people who had spoken about the health center budget returned to their seats.

Mayor Humphrey turned the microphone over to the loud-mouthed Adrian Gangle, who sat on the other side of Mr. Dingle. Marti had noticed the two men occasionally whisper to each other. She figured they agreed on a lot of money issues.

Gangle gave a broad smile that Marti thought looked more condescending than friendly. "Now folks, we all want a safe city."

Gene raised his voice, "Some of us want to know the people keeping us safe."

As a few other people voiced agreement, Marti glanced over her shoulder at Chief Friedman and Tony. They stared ahead, saying nothing.

"As I was saying," Gangle continued, "the Police Department budget for rent, salaries, and equipment is $622,000 per year. Add the city's contribution to the pension system and it's more than $800,000."

Dingle leaned to the mic. "Pretty nice pensions, huh?"

Gangle frowned, as if he didn't want to share his time with the mic.

Mayor Humphrey pulled a mic toward her. "As many of you know, the city is forced to contribute more than what we need now to make up for underfunded contributions in the past. Underfunding that occurred before I became mayor, in part because of mistaken budget estimates. That's why we now have a budget director."

"Just sayin'," Dingle said.

Gangle spoke more loudly. "The point is that we have the option of contracting with the county sheriff for protective services. For a fee, of course, but it would end up a lot less than we're paying now." He gestured to the large graph with the most lines, and Marti tuned him out for a minute.

The voice that interrupted her wandering mind was Skelly's. "Most of us are here to give you people our opinion, not hear yours. The paper printed all your graphs and positions."

The mayor glanced at a piece of paper in front of her. "Dr. Hutton, I believed you signed the comment request sheet first. Why don't you come to the table?"

Marti never thought of Skelly as Dr. Hutton. She didn't even remember his first name. As Skelly made his way to the table, her phone vibrated.

Nick's text asked, "Are the blowhards finished yet?"

Marti almost giggled as she typed, "Far from it." Not that she thought Skelly was a blowhard.

Tony Calderone stood from his seat and walked toward the front of the room. Marti knew the tall officer had been with the department more than twenty years. He sat next to Skelly, who had unfolded a piece of paper as big as the charts. He clipped it to one of the easels in the front of the room.

Marti squinted. At the top of Skelly's graph were the words "Response Time Versus Distance." Skelly sat and placed a paper on the table in front of him.

"Officer Calderone?" the Mayor asked.

Tony nodded. "Dr. Hutton asked me to sit beside him, in case you have questions that require my expertise rather than his."

"I see," she said.

Skelly acted as if he had paid no attention to either of them. "Thank you, Madam Mayor, council members."

Mr. Dingle sat up straighter, but said nothing.

"As you know, I serve as the county coroner, an elected position, the person who certifies the cause of death in certain circumstances. I also work part time in the hospital ER and serve as its medical examiner. In the latter capacity, I examine many of those who die or are brought to the hospital after death, to find the information needed to determine the cause of death."

Dingle leaned forward. "So, two paychecks, then?"

"Since you aren't a county official, Mr. Dingle, you may not be aware that the coroner does not receive a salary unless he or she spends more than ten hours per month on the duties of the office. That amount of time is rare."

Gene again raised his voice. "Afraid you're getting short-changed, Dingle?"

Several people tittered.

Even Marti knew the long-serving city clerk never liked being corrected. About anything.

Skelly continued. "When I'm called to the scene of an accident or crime, I'm one of the first on the scene. Logland police officers, and maybe EMTs, have preceded me."

"Now the sheriff..." Dingle began.

Mayor Humphrey spoke sharply. "Let the man speak."

"Minutes matter in examining the deceased," Skelly said, "and I cannot do more than look at someone until the police have inspected the victim and said it's okay for me to disturb a crime scene. Most people in this county live in Logland, and most crimes are committed here. The sheriff and his deputies cover almost 800 hundred square miles. At night – I know because I asked – there are usually two or three sheriff deputies on patrol."

A female council member – Marti thought she was a retired school teacher – said, "I don't think it's more than two unless the weather's really bad."

"Could be," Skelly said.

Gangle leaned forward and Skelly held up a hand. "Given the size of our county, a deputy could easily be thirty or forty miles away. If they are responding to another call, they can't leave that scene immediately. That means the EMTs and I will arrive first. If they cannot render aid, they will leave and the corpse and I will await a sheriff deputy."

Alice said, "Ugh," really loudly.

Dingle smiled broadly, but without humor. "Are you afraid of the dark, Dr. Hutton?"

No one laughed.

"I'm afraid of losing the kind of time that would enable law enforcement to catch a killer, among other factors. If a body warms or cools, it's harder to establish the time of death. I can provide more examples if need be."

Gangle frowned. "One of our concerns is professionalism, Dr. Hutton. It takes a lot of training to keep police officers up-to-date on skills or equipment. The sheriff holds a training event each month."

In an impassive tone, Skelly asked, "Are you asking me a question or just making a statement."

Gangle flushed. "I'm curious about your opinion as to the skills of the members of the Logland Police Department. You've probably interacted with all of them at one time or another."

"Always professional, and I'm aware of a number of occasions when one or more officers has attended training up in Springfield, or down in Carlinville."

Not bothering with the mic, Dingle said, "And that costs money."

Skelly turned to Calderone. "You do a certain amount here, don't you?"

Tony nodded. "When one of us attends a formal course, we bring back the materials and do what the chief calls in-service sessions for the other officers. I don't charge when I do that."

Low laughter came from around the room.

Marti thought it would be fair to say Mr. Dingle bared his teeth as he looked at Skelly and asked, "And do you find Chief Friedman to be competent?"

Marti turned her head, but Chief Friedman showed no reaction. *Good for her.*

"Very," Skelly said.

"And you would know, wouldn't you, Dr. Hutton?" Dingle asked.

Even though Marti was behind him, there was no missing that Skelly squared his shoulders and sat up straighter. "Excuse me?"

"You two are in bed together on a lot of levels, aren't you?"

Skelly stood in a fluid motion and tried to launch himself across the table, on his stomach, arms stretched toward Dingle.

Tony grabbed Skelly's belt and pulled him back to his chair.

Several people stood. A man called, "Go get 'em, Skelly!"

The mayor pounded her gavel, hard. "Please have a seat! Everyone."

Skelly stayed standing, glaring at Dingle.

"Uh, Dr. Hutton," the mayor said, "did you want to add anything else?"

Skelly nodded to her. "I believe I've contributed what I can."

He turned away from the council and mayor, walked rapidly down the center aisle, and banged the huge wooden door as he left the courtroom. His exodus gave people a chance to turn their heads toward the back, and many eyes rested on Chief Friedman, who had not left her seat. She nodded pleasantly at a couple of people.

Marti marveled at her calm. *I want to be just like her.*

The mayor banged her gavel again, but not as hard. "Chief Friedman. I have a couple of questions."

As others sat, the chief stood. "Certainly." She moved to the aisle and toward the front, taking the seat Skelly had just vacated.

Tony turned his head slightly toward her and nodded as the chief sat down.

Marti swore Tony was trying not to grin.

"Thank you, Chief Friedman," the mayor said. "Perhaps you can offer your thoughts on response time if we have no local station."

"Of course. Since we work only in town, one of our officers can usually be at any scene in three to four minutes."

"Even at night?" Gangle asked.

"Between nine PM and six AM, it's possible the one officer on duty could be at a car accident when the rare break-in call comes in. When I came to Logland four years ago, we began a night system of officers on call. They can be on scene much faster than a sheriff deputy, who could be miles away."

Before Gangle could respond, Dingle pulled the mic from him. "How fast?"

"When officers are on call, they commit to being out the door within one minute after the county's central 9-1-1 dispatch contacts them. Most of us keep coats at bedside and a car in a garage so we don't have to scrape snow."

Gangle took back the mic. "What do your officers earn for sleeping?"

Marti saw Elizabeth's shoulders stiffen. "No more than you, sir. No one gets paid unless they take a call."

Several people tittered, and Marti giggled out loud.

Dingle smirked. "And what if…"

Before he could finish the question, Squeaky Miller stood. "I want to know what Louella Belle Simpson was doing in my laundromat the day she died. She never did her laundry in my place. Why was she there?"

Dingle leaned forward. "That's police business, Mr. Miller, not a topic for a public meeting."

Chief Friedman spoke loudly and clearly. "My full report has been submitted to the mayor and council members, and I believe they plan to make it public."

Dingle started to say something else, but the mayor said, "Let her speak."

"Louella Belle Simpson was in the laundromat at the request of City Clerk Donald Dingle. Unknown to me, he had asked her to tell him why more college students seemed to be going in and out of the laundromat."

Elizabeth stared at Dingle. "Had she not been asked to go to your laundromat, Mr. Miller, she'd likely be alive today."

CHAPTER TWO

TUESDAY MORNING, ELIZABETH stirred cream into her coffee and looked out the window next to her booth in the Bully Pulpit. The day's anticipated afternoon thunderstorm would probably not be as loud as the prior night's budget hearing after she explained Dingle's role in Louella Belle Simpson's presence in the laundromat last December.

When the room had quieted, none of the council members asked what she meant. Elizabeth knew they'd read her report, and she thought at least one of them would comment. *What did Donald Dingle have on members of the City Council?* She didn't care. Her focus had been on keeping the police force on duty in Logland.

She hadn't thought anyone other than Dingle and his buddy Councilman Gangle believed the sheriff should patrol Logland. But she had wanted it on the record that since she'd become chief a few years ago, crime was down.

Especially violent crime. Not that Logland was a hotbed of bar fights, drug busts, or liquor store robberies. Still, crime continued to drop and she had increased patrol hours without adding officers. She'd made all those points last night.

When had life gotten so complicated? She'd left Chicago at age thirty-two to get away from some of the most heinous crimes and have fewer people prying into her private life.

Crime, even murder, still happened in small towns like Logland, but until now she had thought her personal life was her own. Dingle not only decided to make part of it public, he was wrong about her and Skelly. They'd become good friends, but not – to use Skelly's line – friends with benefits. She knew he would like to be just that. She wasn't sure. He made her laugh, but...

Whoosh!

The Bully Pulpit's glass door blew open with the March breeze. Skelly ran fingers through his black hair to undo some of the wind's damage, and pointed at Elizabeth with his other hand. He came to the red vinyl booth and slid in across from her.

"Sorry I'm late. My early-bird sister called from Phoenix. She has Google set to notify her if my name comes up in a news story."

Elizabeth smiled. "If I'd known that, I'd have planted some."

Skelly picked up the laminated menu. "Funny. Did you order?"

"Yes. And I ordered you two eggs, sunny side up, with toast and bacon."

He grinned. "That'll get people talking."

She shrugged. "Let them talk."

Skelly eyed Elizabeth's dark blue uniform jacket. "Why are you in full garb instead of your usual blazer and slacks?"

"I figure last night's tussle could have more media than Jerry Pew looking for me today." Elizabeth took that day's *Logland Press* from the booth bench beside her and plopped it on the table. "Speaking of Jerry, I had no idea he could switch out a front page photo that fast."

Skelly pulled the paper toward him. "Crud. I didn't have time to go online to look. My sister did, of course."

Elizabeth smirked as he studied the photo, which showed Skelly sliding across the table toward Dingle, hands outstretched. Calderone leaned toward Skelly to grab his belt. The caption read, "Heated discussion at City Council meeting. More on our website."

Skelly groaned. "What was I thinking?"

"That you wanted to strangle him. Luckily, you didn't get that far. Calderone or I would've had to haul your tailbone to the station."

Skelly pushed the paper back toward Elizabeth. "At least they didn't talk about your bombshell about Dingle and Louella Belle. You'd have been there all night."

Elizabeth raised her coffee mug as if toasting him. "The mayor said she'd release all the information and they can discuss it at the next meeting if they need to. Besides, Jerry gave it lots of attention on the paper's website. I'll be surprised if Dingle doesn't have a stroke."

"Think he'll try to chop less from your budget?" Skelly asked.

"You don't know Dingle very well. He'll find a way to get back at me."

Nick ambled over from the cash register, where he'd just finished handing a departing customer his change. "Hey, you guys. Are you really shacking up?"

Elizabeth threw back her head and laughed as Skelly put his forehead on the Formica-topped booth table.

Marti's voice boomed from behind the diner's serving counter. "Nick! You can't ask stuff like that!"

Nick reddened and stammered. "Sorry. Everybody asks, so I thought you'd rather me tell 'em the truth."

Skelly sat up and Elizabeth wiped her eyes with a napkin. "Friends, Nick. Just friends." She glanced at Skelly. They had talked about something more, but she didn't want a personal relationship with someone she had a professional one with. He said he would wear her down. He might, but not anytime soon.

Skelly grinned. "Seriously, Nick, thanks for the thought."

Elizabeth threw her now balled-up napkin at Skelly. "Nick, I could use a warm-up on coffee."

"Food ready?" Skelly asked.

"I've got it." Marti came toward them with a round tray that held two large plates of food.

Nick sidestepped her. "I'll get the coffee."

As Marti placed a plate in front of Elizabeth, a sausage rolled off. She picked it up and took a bite.

"I'll get another one," Marti said. "Don't eat that one."

"No worries," Elizabeth said, as she chewed.

"Ten-second rule." Skelly stabbed an egg yolk with his fork so it oozed onto his toast.

Marti glanced toward the kitchen. "I'm sorry about that. You know Nick doesn't mean any harm."

"Not a problem," Skelly said.

Elizabeth frowned. "His asking us isn't the problem. It's that people are asking him."

Marti looked away for a second, then back. "Not too many."

The front door whooshed again and Squeaky Miller, in shirtsleeves and minus a jacket, entered. He made his way to their booth. "Hey Chief. I'm sorry I brought up Louella Belle Simpson last night."

Elizabeth didn't slide over to make room for him. "There've been a lot of rumors. I wanted to let people know what Dingle did, but I couldn't bring it up. You did me a favor."

Squeaky straightened his shoulders. "That's good. I didn't want to get under your skin, Chief."

Skelly swallowed a huge bite of toast that he had dipped in yolk. "You didn't know Dingle had asked Louella Belle Simpson to watch your laundromat?"

Squeaky shook his head. "I heard all kinds of stuff." He looked at Elizabeth. "Can't you arrest him or something?"

Elizabeth wished she could tell him she'd talked to the local state's attorney, Xavier Donaldson, who could think of no crime beyond stupidity. Donaldson would flip out if his comment got around town. "Nope. He didn't threaten her with anything if she didn't go. Louella Belle was there of her own free will."

"Too bad." Squeaky glanced at Skelly and grinned. "Nice sliding."

"I needed the exercise."

Nick appeared with a glass pot of coffee. "Made some fresh. You want any, Mr. Miller?" Nick reached for Elizabeth's mug.

"No, I have to check the change machine in the laundromat, and I left the dry cleaner's open. Just saw the chief and came over for a second." He gave Elizabeth a mock salute and left.

Elizabeth glanced around the diner. Cookie shop owner Doris sat in a booth on the far side of the diner, eating breakfast and reading the paper. A man she didn't know sat near Doris, but the morning rush had been over for a few minutes. Good thing. Elizabeth didn't want the world to hear her talking about Dingle's comments.

Skelly wiped his fingers on a napkin. "Why in the hell are Dingle and his buddy Gangle so intent on getting rid of the police force?"

"My guess is because they can't control us. A lot of other departments report to Dingle. I report to the mayor, and through her to the Council. He can't pick up the phone and tell me what to do."

Nick, no longer red-faced, returned to the kitchen and Elizabeth reached into her uniform jacket's pocket to get money for payment and a tip.

"You have to leave?" Skelly asked. "I wanted to talk about…"

Doris' raised voice came from her booth. "Elizabeth! Chief! You won't believe what happened."

Elizabeth gestured with her phone, which had just buzzed, indicating a text. "Come over here and tell us."

She glanced at her text from Sergeant Hammer. "Dingle collapsed in the mayor's office. Ambulance just left City Hall for the hospital."

She turned the phone so Skelly could see the screen. "Hope we don't have to arrest the mayor."

Skelly threw a ten on the table and Elizabeth moved her coffee mug to sit atop her bills as Doris reached their booth. "Chief, did you hear about Mr. Dingle?"

"Just had a text from the station." She gestured that Doris should move aside so she could get out of the booth. "Heading to the hospital now."

Saying nothing, Skelly jogged out ahead of her.

"Does that mean Mr. Dingle is dead?" Doris asked.

Elizabeth smiled as she picked up her hat from the booth seat. "Skelly does a couple shifts a week in the ER. He's probably going over to see if he can help."

Doris cocked her head. "I'm not sure Mr. Dingle would want Skelly's help."

As Elizabeth reached the exit, she heard Marti tell Nick, "See, they each paid for their own breakfast. That's how you know they aren't dating."

ELIZABETH DROVE TO THE hospital without lights and sirens. By the time she got to the edge of town her mind had weighed a lot of alternatives – none of them positive for Donald Dingle. Stroke? Heart attack? Brain aneurism?

She entered the austere ER waiting lounge and looked at the receptionist.

The woman shook her braided red hair. "Nothing yet. The mayor's over there." She pointed to a grouping of chairs in the corner.

Mayor Humphrey sat alone, one hand over her eyes, her shoulders shaking. She looked up as Elizabeth walked over. "You heard?" She sniffed noisily.

Elizabeth sat next to her, and smiled. "Did you deck him?"

"Of course not. We were arguing. Well, he was yelling about last night's meeting, and then he got a funny look. I thought maybe he'd throw up. And he went to the floor, kind of kneeling, then falling face first."

Elizabeth winced. "Hope he didn't break a cheekbone or his nose, on top of whatever else it was."

"My office just got carpeted last year." She blew her nose on a crumpled tissue, then rubbed the back of her neck. "I have such a headache."

"No crime in arguing with an obnoxious colleague, Madam Mayor."

"I was angry. I'd even told him I didn't need the council's approval to fire him, but I didn't say a damn thing about wanting him in a coffin."

Elizabeth smiled. "Out loud, you mean."

"It's not funny!"

Elizabeth sobered. "Of course not. I might have some Tylenol in my car. For your headache."

Humphrey shook her head. "I'm sorry. It's just so awful." She picked her purse off the floor. "I have something to take."

Elizabeth nodded toward the far end of the ER waiting room. "There are small cups next to the fountain. I'll get you some water."

"Thank you."

The brief walk gave Elizabeth time to take in the mayor's demeanor. It would have been awful to see someone collapse in front of her. Still, she was surprised that the woman would sit in the hospital waiting room crying.

Humphrey had been widowed not long before Elizabeth moved to Logland. Maybe Dingle's situation brought back bad memories. She filled the paper cup with water and went back to the mayor.

"Here you go, Sharon. Sorry I can't offer you something stronger." Elizabeth sat down again.

Humphrey popped two white pills in her mouth and drank the water in one gulp. "I'm sorry I snapped at you."

"No problem. I'm glad the EMTs could help him."

Humphrey nodded. "He was unconscious but breathing. When the EMTs put an oxygen mask on him he came to a little."

"Good sign."

The automatic doors opened and Jerry Pew hurried in, eyes on the receptionist.

"Put your shades on, Mayor," Elizabeth said. "Our favorite publisher will write some loathsome bit about your face being tear-stained."

Mayor Humphrey dug in her purse for sunglasses and lipstick while Elizabeth watched Jerry try to wheedle information from the receptionist. She apparently gave him the party line on patient privacy, because Jerry wore an expression of irritation as he turned to leave.

His eyes fell on Elizabeth and the mayor. "Looky who beat me here."

Elizabeth didn't think anyone else in town could get away with saying "looky," but Jerry was pushing seventy-five. He held out a hand and Elizabeth shook it.

"You ladies know how Mr. Dingle's doing?"

Mayor Humphrey stood and extended her hand. "Several people were in the office, so you probably heard he collapsed when we were talking. I don't know anything else. Except that he was alive when the ambulance took him away."

Jerry frowned. "You see him here?"

"No, Jerry, and I'm not family, so I'm not sure I could until he's in a room ready for visitors."

Behind Jerry, Elizabeth saw Skelly open the door from the ER treatment section, see Jerry, and pull the door shut again. She hoped he would come out after Jerry left so they could find out what he knew.

Jerry took a business card from his trouser pocket and passed it to Mayor Humphrey. "I think you have my cell phone, but in case you don't. Call me when you know something."

The mayor made no promise. She glanced at the card as Jerry left the ER, then at Elizabeth. "Getting pretty formal, isn't he?"

"He doesn't want to get scooped. Can I get you some more water or something?"

Humphrey shook her head. "I'm feeling better, I...oh, look. Dr. Hutton."

Skelly came to them and sat in one of the uncomfortable waiting room chairs. Elizabeth and Mayor Humphrey sat down again.

"How is he?" Humphrey asked.

"Lucky to be alive. Can't tell you much, but as he's a public figure and you're the mayor, I'll let you know he probably had a mild heart attack. I see stents in his future."

"But you didn't see him, did you?" Elizabeth asked. She thought that could give Dingle a second heart attack.

Skelly grinned. "I'm not crazy. But I did want to reduce his stress level."

"Good of you." Elizabeth doubted the mayor could hear the sarcasm in her tone.

"That's nice," Humphrey said. "Did you get him flowers in the gift shop?"

Skelly laughed. "Not hardly. I drew a smiley face on some copy paper and had a nurse bring it in to him. I wrote 'get well' and signed it 'the ME and the PC.'"

Elizabeth groaned and Mayor Humphrey's eyes widened. "Did he see it?"

"The nurse who delivered it said he smiled at it. I was going to write something about staying out of my part of the hospital, but I figured he might not get it."

Humphrey stared, her expression a question.

"Stay out of the autopsy rooms," Skelly said.

AS ELIZABETH WALKED BEHIND THE counter that separated the police station bullpen from the public waiting area, Sergeant Hammer handed her a stack of phone messages. "Your voice mailbox is full again."

Elizabeth groaned. "I finally had all the messages off my phone. You have these in order of importance?"

"I think so. Ms. Maitlin, one of the admin people in the mayor's office, is on top. She can't get hold of the mayor and wants to know if you heard anything."

Elizabeth handed that message back to Hammer. "You can tell her I didn't see him, but I know he's conscious and able to smile. And tell her the mayor's fine. She was still in the waiting room when I left the hospital, and cell service sucks in the hospital."

"You know more?"

Elizabeth nodded. "Skelly said he sees stents in Dingle's future, but we can't repeat that."

Corporal Mahan looked up from where he was writing in the police blotter. "So, heart attack?"

Calderone entered the bullpen from the hallway. "Can't be. He's the tinman."

"Nah," Hammer said. "Not thin enough."

"Gentlemen." When their expressions indicated they weren't sure if she was joining in or suggesting they stop berating Dingle, she grinned, "Play nice. He does influence our budget."

Elizabeth had half-turned toward her office when she saw Calderone and Mahan exchange a look. Mahan said, "The thing is, the more he talks about it, the more likely it is some of the guys will look for other jobs."

She faced them. "Is anyone seriously looking?"

Both men shrugged.

"You guys aren't usually shy."

Hammer spoke from his desk. "I don't think anyone has job apps out, but people talk about it." He nodded toward Calderone. "Some of the old farts could retire, but…"

Calderone broke in. "Most of the younger farts don't want to move, or even work for the sheriff if we get axed and the county hires more deputies. Too much driving on bad roads all winter."

Mahan nodded. "Yeah. But you know how it is. The Illinois Pension Code covers all municipal police officers in one system. Somebody could go to Taylorville or Carlinville and not miss a beat."

Elizabeth leaned against Hammer's desk. "I need a Tums."

Hammer laughed. "The mayor's on your side, and I don't think many council members want to wait thirty minutes if someone steals their cars. Sorry, no Tums."

She stood up straight. "Okay, I'll fortify with some coffee. I've got a pile of messages."

Mahan grinned. "You'll need more Tums if you drink coffee."

"Put a cork in it," Elizabeth said.

"Wine *would* be better," Hammer said.

Elizabeth ignored him and stopped by the break room to grab a cup of coffee to replace the one she didn't finish at the Bully Pulpit. Before she started on the pile of messages, she sat staring at the phone on her desk.

How could she not have known some of her officers were concerned enough to think about applying for other jobs? Aloud, she said, "I hope Dingle has to retire."

Within half-an-hour she'd returned a bunch of calls -- evenly divided between congratulations on taking down Dingle at the council meeting and inquiring about his health -- and given the rest of the stack to Hammer to handle.

Elizabeth had begun reviewing the batch of incident reports from last night when her phone buzzed. When Hammer put a call through directly it meant it was the mayor or Skelly. She picked up the receiver. "Good news, I hope?"

Skelly snorted. "As a doctor I should say yes. Bottom line, Mr. Dingle is en route to the Cardiac Cath Lab for what Dr. Prasad thinks will be three stents. If they get in there and don't like what they see, he'll need a bypass. They'd probably send him to Springfield."

"If you find out how it goes, let me know."

"I'll stop by the Recovery Room about the time he should be in there."

"Better stay out of his line of sight or he'll have another heart attack."

Skelly snorted. "Let me think about that."

"Can I let people know?" Elizabeth asked.

"I heard the mayor asking Dr. Prasad a couple questions so she could do a press release, so I'd say yes. Lunch?"

"I'm backed up here. Contrary to some people's opinions, we do a lot of work."

"Catch you later." Skelly hung up.

Elizabeth went back to the reports, frowning as she read. Most nights they had no more than speeding tickets on the highway, unless it was high school or college homecoming, or

Halloween. At eleven-fifteen last night one homeowner reported an iPad taken from an unlocked car in their driveway.

Between six and seven-thirty this morning four more people who lived near the college called about thefts from cars. Three cars had been left unlocked, with glove boxes and trunk rifled. Two of the four had no more than change taken, one a portable GPS device.

A fifth call came from the college president himself, who said he thought he locked his car, but couldn't swear to it. That made Elizabeth wonder if a thief was after something specific. Pretty ballsy to target a car that was parked in the circular driveway in front of President Dodd's large, on-campus residence.

Dodd's call had been taken as the day shift came on, so Calderone had gone to campus himself. His note indicated that Wally Kermit, everyone's favorite campus security officer, had been irritated Dodd had called Logland Police in addition to the campus unit.

Elizabeth buzzed Hammer. "Calderone in the station?"

"Nope. Supposedly someone 'shifty' has been hanging around the gas station at the edge of town. He went to check. Help you?"

"Why did Dodd call us?"

"He had a briefcase in the car. He wants us to keep an eye out for it."

"He thinks someone would leave it on a park bench?"

"Calderone said Dodd was more irritated at himself than the thief. He was kind of talking to himself when he said, 'Never should have left that in the stupid car.'"

"If it gets turned in, let me know." Elizabeth studied the list of the briefcase's contents. Draft of a new policy on fraternal organizations on campus, assorted writing implements – he couldn't just say pens? – and personnel papers.

"Ah, personnel papers." If they dealt with specific employees, leaving that material in the car was stupid. *Who at the university would reprimand its president?*

Final Operation

ELIZABETH HAD FINISHED a late lunch at her desk when Hammer's raised voice drifed in from the bullpen. "You gotta be kidding! When?"

She stood and walked quickly to him. "What?"

Wide-eyed, Hammer hung up. "Donald Dingle. They got him to his private room and he died ten minutes later."

CHAPTER THREE

ELIZABETH HADN'T WISHED DONALD Dingle would drop dead more than a couple dozen times. And never out loud. But now that he had, why did it have to be the day after she called him out at a City Council meeting? To say nothing of Skelly trying to grab him by the throat.

The Tuesday afternoon thunderstorm kicking into gear had made the road slick with the mix of water and oil that coated the road at the beginning of every rainfall. She didn't drive fast or turn on the Crown Vic's siren as she drove the mile to the hospital. The only timing consideration was finding out details so she knew them before the gossip mongers' tongues wagged.

When she walked into the hospital lobby, it appeared word had not spread. A candy-striper pushed a three-tiered cart with items from the gift shop, en route to sell sundries and magazines to patients. The front desk receptionist gave Elizabeth a cheery wave. As the elevator door opened, a nurse exited with a new mom and baby in a wheelchair, followed by a dad who looked as if he'd been gob smacked.

Elizabeth got in and pushed the button for the third-floor cardiac unit. Dingle's body might have been moved, but staff on the unit could tell her what happened. They generally were more forthcoming after a death than they were for a living patient.

The cardiac floor never had the bustle of pediatrics or even general surgery, but today Elizabeth did not hear even the squeak of a gurney's wheels or see the flash of a patient call light. She walked down the hall to the nurse's station at the far end of the floor.

A physician sat between two nurses, eyes intent on a computer screen. The older nurse, a man who often half-jogged through the hallways, pointed at the screen. "See, all the meds were administered before he left Recovery."

The younger nurse, a woman Elizabeth didn't know well, said, "Dr. Prasad, I checked the IV. He had moved his arm, so I undid a kink. His color was good."

Elizabeth cleared her throat. "Sorry to interrupt."

Dr. Prasad nodded and both nurses said, "Hey, Chief."

"Thought I'd check in for a minute. It's never easy when someone dies on your watch."

Dr. Prasad nodded again. "Everything went well in the Cardiac Cath Lab. But at his age, sometimes a body doesn't handle even stents as well as a younger patient."

"Sure. I wouldn't ordinarily stop by. Given his prominence, Mayor Humphrey and I will get a lot of calls."

The nurses had turned so she could see their badges. Jeffrey said, "The mayor just left. She seemed kind of shaken. We made her sit in the family waiting room with a cup of coffee for a few minutes."

"She was with him?"

"Just briefly," Jeffrey said.

"I'm glad he wasn't alone," Elizabeth said.

The younger nurse, Mary Beth, wrinkled her nose. "She said she would sit in his room for a few minutes in case he woke up. She was texting on her phone when I looked in there."

Elizabeth glanced from one nurse to the other. "When did you learn there could be a problem? Did she call you in?"

Jeffrey nodded. "Probably not eight or ten minutes later she walked into the hall and hollered for a nurse. I got there first and she pointed in the room and said he was breathing slower, I think that's what she said."

"So he was dead when you got to his room?" Elizabeth asked.

"I'd say taking his last breath or two," Jeffrey said.

Dr. Prasad spoke up. "He had a DNR -- an order not to resuscitate."

All three nodded.

"You don't need an autopsy in a situation like that, do you?" Elizabeth asked.

"Generally, no," Dr. Prasad said.

Generally?

"He's downstairs," Jeffrey said. "Skelly'll hand him off to Gretchen and her people."

A cynical thought crossed Elizabeth's mind. Gretchen, owner of Leaving the Farm Funeral Home, loved a big crowd. She'd once told Elizabeth a large service was better than a full-page ad in the *Logland Press.*

"He always said he never wanted to retire," Elizabeth said.

When they said nothing, she added, "I'll head out. Thanks for talking to me." They hadn't, really. They also hadn't said they thought his death was anything but natural. That was all she cared about.

Elizabeth took the elevator to the ground level in search of Skelly. The green-tiled walls and black-and-white photos of the hospital that lined the top half of the walls gave the hallway a 1950s appearance. Skelly had said several times he doubted the hospital would ever upgrade the basement level, which housed only the medical examiner/autopsy space and one lab.

Skelly kept the door to his space locked, so Elizabeth knocked. The man who opened the door was not the jovial Skelly she usually saw.

"What is it?" she asked.

"Come in." He gestured that she should follow him through the small waiting room into his work area. "I don't like this."

"You mean you like some deaths but not others?"

"Funny. Plenty of deaths are sudden. But anytime someone goes from perfect surgery to dead in a few minutes, I want answers."

From the edge of the immaculate autopsy room, Elizabeth studied Donald Dingle. He lay on the steel examination table, covered in a sheet, with only his head exposed. No matter how often she saw a body, she was always surprised at how quickly the color left a corpse's face. "Are you going to conduct an autopsy?"

"I've asked Dr. Prasad to come down." As Skelly said this, someone knocked on the door. He pointed to the waiting area. "Can you hang around out there for a few minutes?"

If the cardiologist was surprised to see Elizabeth, he didn't show it. "Chief."

"Dr. Prasad. I'll wait out here while you two talk."

Prasad looked from Skelly to Elizabeth. "Why don't you join us? Not in the discussion, just in the room."

Skelly's expression was unreadable.

"Sure. Everything okay?" Elizabeth asked.

"Why wouldn't it be?" Prasad asked.

Elizabeth avoided saying she inquired first and followed the two men into the autopsy room.

Dr. Prasad handed Skelly a folder he had carried under his left arm. "We can't access the Recovery Room data from the floor, so I had them bring down some printed material." The two doctors opened the file and spread the few sheets of paper on the second, vacant, steel examination table. They said nothing for a full minute.

"He looked great," Skelly said. "Strong blood pressure as soon as he came out of sedation."

"It's pretty light sedation," Prasad said.

"True," Skelly said. "Pulse, temperature, alertness. I stopped by Recovery, you know. Before he was awake."

"I heard," Prasad said.

Elizabeth thought his noncommittal tone said more than his words.

"You had post-mortem bloodwork done?"

Prasad glanced at Skelly and back at the papers. "Yes. You spoke to the nurse in Recovery, I believe."

"Yeah I rarely go up there, but I checked on him in the ER, too. He and I had an almost-tussle last night."

Prasad smiled. "I believe few people in town are unaware."

"Damn Jerry Pew." Skelly gathered the papers and put them back in the folder. "What do you think? Ordinarily I'd send him straight to the funeral home."

"In this case," Prasad began.

Pounding on the suite door interrupted him.

"Jeez." Skelly raised his voice. "Coming."

He hurried through the waiting room, opened the door, and stepped back.

Elizabeth couldn't see who stood in the doorway, but Skelly seemed surprised to see them.

"Mayor, Tony." Skelly glanced at Elizabeth and Dr. Prasad. "What's up?"

As they entered, a petite woman in rose surgical scrubs followed them.

Still appearing puzzled, Skelly turned to Elizabeth. "This is Norma Norton. She was Mr. Dingle's Recovery Room nurse."

Calderone spoke. "Skelly, Dr. Hutton, I've been asked to insist you not conduct an autopsy on Mr. Dingle."

Elizabeth spoke sharply. "Asked by whom?"

"Me," Mayor Humphrey said. "There has been an allegation that Dr. Hutton may have inserted something into Mr. Dingle's IV."

Skelly's voice rose. "Who the hell said that?"

Norton spoke. "I wondered why you stopped by Recovery. When I found the extra syringe on a counter, I figured out why."

No one said anything for two or three seconds. Elizabeth spoke first. "Do you have more than that, Ms. Norton?"

The anger in Norton's expression made her appear older than her approximately forty years. "What more do you need?"

"Gee," Elizabeth said, "evidence of some sort."

Mayor Humphrey cleared her throat. "Chief, I believe we need to turn this over to the Illinois State Police…"

Elizabeth interrupted her. "If you are trying to imply that the Logland Police Department is not sufficiently professional to investigate a man with whom we work, you would be wrong." She tilted her head toward Calderone. "Have Dr. Hutton ride to the station with you. I'll be right behind you."

Skelly turned to Dr. Prasad. "Mr. Dingle needs to be placed in one of the cold chambers. One of the EMTs who works out of the Emergency Room would know how to do that."

"Yes, Doctor," Prasad said. He didn't move.

Skelly's expression became impassive as he looked at Mayor Humphrey. "Do you mind if I get my jacket, or are you afraid I'm hiding some kind of weapon?"

Humphrey flushed, and Calderone said, "I'll get it from your office."

He walked toward Skelly's private office, which was to the left of the autopsy room.

Elizabeth turned to Norton. "Officer Mahan will be here soon and he'll drive you to the station for your statement."

Norton squared her shoulders. "What do you mean *my* statement?" She pointed at Skelly. "He's the murderer."

Elizabeth would thoroughly investigate Norton's allegation, but she would need a lot more substance before she would act on it. "You can put your finger down. If you watch much television, you know police start the investigative process after an accusation, then move to evidence and, when possible, corroboration. Is your shift finished? I can have Officer Mahan meet you wherever you have your purse."

As Norton sputtered, Calderone returned with Skelly's faux-suede jacket and handed it to him. He looked at Elizabeth. "Cuffs?"

"Not on this level of information. Have Mahan bring over an evidence bag to collect the syringe."

Calderone nodded, and Elizabeth deliberately didn't meet Skelly's eyes. The two men left.

Elizabeth turned to Norton. "The syringe is secure where you left it? Someone has been charged with guarding it?"

"Well, no. I mean, I left it on a tray on the counter, where Mr. Dingle was." Her voice trailed off.

"You wha...?" Elizabeth stopped herself so she didn't yell. She walked the few steps to a phone that sat on the always-unoccupied reception desk. "Ms. Norton. Call up to the Recovery Room to be sure that tray is where you left it, and no one touches it. You and I will proceed up there as soon as your call is done."

Elizabeth picked up the receiver. When Norton didn't move toward her, she gestured with it. "Come on. You can talk faster than we can take the elevator. Tell them we're on our way."

Norton took the receiver and Elizabeth walked a few steps from her. She would give the woman the illusion of some privacy, but she'd catch every word.

As Norton told the hospital operator to connect her to Recovery, Elizabeth turned to Humphrey, whose complexion had returned to normal. "We'll need a statement from you, Madam Mayor. I'd like to get Dr. Hutton's and Ms. Norton's first, since I assume you weren't a witness."

"Elizabeth, I..."

"You could make some notes, while it's fresh in your mind." Elizabeth turned her head toward Norton.

The nurse's voice had dropped very low. "What do you mean? I didn't tell you to do that!" Norton listened for a few seconds. "We're on the way back there. Don't touch anything else."

She replaced the phone and turned to Elizabeth and Mayor Humphrey. "Um. Nurse Werner, um, cleaned the area."

"Where did she put the syringe?" Elizabeth asked.

"In the sharps box."

Elizabeth felt her frustration mount. On one hand, contaminated evidence could make it impossible to prosecute Skelly. On the other, the uncertainty created could destroy his reputation.

CHAPTER FOUR

ELIZABETH STARED AT NORTON. "The box holds used syringes and needles, doesn't it?"

Norton nodded. "We can get a key to open the box."

Elizabeth turned to Mayor Humphrey. "Do you have direct knowledge of this situation?"

"No. And Chief, I…"

"I've got this, Mayor. I'll call you with the usual periodic updates."

Dr. Prasad cleared his throat.

He'd been so silent that Elizabeth had forgotten they would be leaving him alone in the suite. "Can you lock up, Dr. Prasad?"

"I'll handle things here." As he turned toward the autopsy room, he stuck his hands in the pockets of his lab coat and walked with his eyes on the floor."

Elizabeth motioned that the two women should precede her into the hall. "Ms. Norton, is there a staff or service elevator?"

"Yes, it's around the corner from the public elevator."

"Let's you and I head for that one."

Elizabeth held the door open so the two women could enter the hall before her. She didn't trust herself to speak to Humphrey.

She'd always found the mayor to be fair-minded, but her seeming rush to judgment in this case could do a lot of damage.

When the three of them reached the public elevator Norton kept going. Elizabeth followed her around the corner and they stopped in front of the large service elevator. After Norton pressed the call button, they stood in silence for about thirty seconds.

As the elevator doors began to open, Norton asked, "What happens now?"

"Here at the hospital, we'll retrieve the syringe, or at least the box of them, and place whatever we get in an evidence bag. Most of our interview with you will take place at the station, but we'll take a few photos of the scene where the alleged crime took place."

Norton flushed. "I know what I found."

Elizabeth stared straight ahead. "I hear you."

They stepped off the slow-moving elevator into the third-floor hallway, whose gleaming floors and subdued wall paint told their location as much as a wheelchair sitting outside a patient room. They turned right, toward double doors that bore a sign saying "Hospital personnel only." Norton held her badge to a metallic plate on the wall, and the button in the middle of it turned from red to green as the doors swung open.

Immediately ahead of them was the area where patients were prepped before surgery. They turned left, and after about fifty yards walked through another set of doors into the Recovery Room.

Elizabeth halted. Unlike the patient prep area, which had individual cubicles, this huge room had perhaps ten curtained spaces, all open. Each held a gurney covered in a white sheet, a pillow on top. No patients remained in the room, and every space appeared to have been tidied, and probably disinfected, after its prior patient

To the right was a small staff area. The only person seated there was a nurse who had been typing something. However, she stopped to stare at the two newcomers.

Elizabeth turned to the woman. "I'm Chief Friedman. Are you Nurse Werner?"

"No, Chief, but I can page her."

"Hang on a minute, would you?"

"Yes, Chief."

To Norton, Elizabeth said, "Which area held Mr. Dingle?"

Norton pointed to a gurney immediately across and two down from them. The space around it had an IV stand and a bedside table on wheels that could be raised and lowered. The wall behind the gurney held connections for oxygen and blood pressure equipment, and a number of items Elizabeth didn't recognize.

Under the wall paraphernalia was a narrow counter space with an equally narrow cabinet below. The only item on top of the counter was the red plastic box with its narrow opening, used for syringe disposal.

Elizabeth had personally worked with the City Council to get the sharps boxes for each restroom in every city building. She advocated for them as a repository for insulin needles. In fact she was more concerned that any illegal drug syringes be placed in them. She didn't want them reused. In the rest rooms, the boxes were larger and affixed to the wall.

"Is this how the space looked when you left it?"

Norton shook her head, and Elizabeth noted her forehead had dampened with perspiration. "I hadn't cleaned up yet. There's a lot of clutter if a patient is with you for a while. The table had some tubing I didn't use, empty cups, at least one roll of paper tape. Lots of stuff."

"Corporal Mahan will go over all of that with you. I suggest you take a minute to envision the scene as it was when you left. Write some notes or draw a diagram if you like." Elizabeth approached the other nurse. "Would you have a piece of paper Ms. Norton could use?"

"Yes, Chief." She turned to a printer, pulled out its paper tray, and selected a couple of sheets. "Will this be enough?"

Elizabeth smiled at her. "Yes, thanks." She handed the paper to Norton as Mahan came in the room. Elizabeth walked to him.

In his patrol uniform, wearing his gun on one hip and night stick on the other, he looked very out of place. "Chief?" He held out the evidence bag.

Elizabeth tilted her head toward Norton. "You'll need it. Start the interview with Ms. Norton and take some pictures of the space. Since it's been cleaned, we won't need too many."

"What's the objective?" he asked, quietly.

"We need to know where she found a syringe, and the condition the space was in when she left it to go to the lobby."

"The lobby?" Mahan asked.

"That's where she ran into the mayor. I guess we don't know where she was going. Ask her."

"Will do." He jotted a couple lines in his notebook.

"Start Ms. Norton's statement here, but bring her down to the station fairly quickly. We'll need permission to remove the box of sharps on that counter, so we can run prints. I have no idea how easy that will be, or if we'll have to involve the city attorney." Elizabeth hoped not. Harold Groff primarily dealt with finances and property rights.

Norton moved closer to them. Her voice had become strained. Elizabeth sensed she was holding back tears. "I don't know why you can't take it."

Elizabeth ignored her and turned to Mahan. "Whoever heads this unit may be able to grant permission. If he or she resists and it looks like it would take too long to wade through everything now, get a commitment to place the box in a locked area. Maybe even a safe in the hospital administrator's office."

"I can handle this," Mahan said. "I'll call you if I need to."

"Good. I'd stick around, but I want to get back to the station." She turned to Norton. "Make your notes."

Elizabeth turned and started to walk out. She stopped and turned. "Mahan."

"Chief?"

Final Operation

"The nurse at the desk can page the nurse who cleaned up the space. Her name's Werner. She may have something important to add."

"Will do." Mahan turned back to Norton.

As Elizabeth got to the swinging door to the hallway, she noted that the nurse who had provided the paper was on the phone. She wanted to tell her not to talk about the police presence, but that could just add to the rumor mill.

She had driven halfway to the station before she realized how tightly she gripped the steering wheel. She loosened her grip and relaxed her shoulders as she rolled to a stop at a traffic light near the town square.

To all eyes but hers, the Logland town square was the same today as yesterday. The three-story, limestone courthouse in the middle of the square still needed the wooden cupola on the top painted. Crocuses dotted the courthouse lawn. Three women Elizabeth guessed to be administrative staff exited the coffee house, each carrying a cup of coffee and small bag that likely held pastries.

The light turned green. She drove by small retail shops and insurance agencies and turned onto the street that would take her to the police station. As usual, her designated parking spot was open – only Dingle had ever pulled into it when she was out. She parked the Crown Vic and made herself walk into the station at a measured pace.

The front entrance was closer to her car, so Elizabeth generally used it. As she entered on the public side of the long counter, Sergeant Hammer stood from behind his desk in the bullpen and approached the counter-height swinging door as she came through it. They both stopped.

"What the hell, Chief?"

"Could be nothing but an incorrect accusation, but we have to check it out. Where are Calderone and Dr. Hutton?"

"In the conference room. Skelly...Dr. Hutton hadn't eaten, so we split the chicken sandwich my wife packed me. Maybe I shouldn't have done that?"

"Good for you." Elizabeth smiled. "We can make no assumptions, but I'd be surprised if the nurse's accusation holds water. A damn shame she made it before contacting hospital security or us."

They moved toward the hall that led to the conference room and other parts of the station. Hammer muttered, "Or at all."

Elizabeth shrugged. "If she really saw something, she had to say so. She may have jumped to a conclusion, but I'm not about to assume that."

As they passed his desk, Hammer asked, "You uh, okay with this?"

Elizabeth pointed an index finger at him. "You're as bad as Nick. Any urgent calls I have to return before I head to Calderone and Sk…Dr. Hutton?"

"I think I handled everything. The mayor asked to be put through to your voice mail."

"Good thing I cleared it out." She headed down the hall.

The atmosphere in the conference room was not as tense as Elizabeth expected. Calderone sat across from Skelly, one long leg draped across the chair next to him. Skelly's expression was stony and his scrubs bore perspiration stains. Elizabeth shut the door and sat next to Calderone.

"Dr. Hutton," she began.

He stiffened.

"If I hadn't asked Calderone to bring you down here, God knows who the mayor would have called or where you'd be right now. Please understand that."

"I told him that," Calderone said.

Skelly's face remained almost expressionless "Why not sort it out there?"

"If she had walked in and asked questions instead of made accusations, I could have handled it that way." She paused. "I will say that I find the possibility of you killing Donald Dingle to be far-fetched."

Skelly attempted a smile. "Like football field far, or here to Springfield?"

Elizabeth smiled tightly. "Let's just say far."

Skelly grew somber.

Elizabeth turned to Calderone. "People will say that I, all of us, are biased in favor of Skelly because we all have friendly relationships. And anyone who goes into the diner knows Skelly and I eat there a lot. You need to be primary on this."

Calderone sat up straighter. "If that's the case, Chief, then I need to ask you to leave the room."

Skelly's eyebrows shot up.

Elizabeth stood. "I figured you'd say that. I want to be kept well-informed." She glanced at Skelly. "I'll ascertain what Nurse Norton believes she saw. You know you're under no obligation to talk to us at this point, right?"

"Do I need a lawyer?" he asked.

"Up to you. Personally, I'd want some chips to fall before I spent the money." She allowed herself to smile. "Could be this will be done quickly. I hope so."

"Out," Calderone said.

"Yes, sir."

Calderone reddened more than she'd ever seen and Skelly's lips twitched. Elizabeth left the conference room.

Voices reached her from the bullpen. She recognized Mahan, Norton, and Hammer, but there was one more male voice. She headed that way.

Norma Norton appeared red-eyed but composed. The tall, black man with her was the hospital's CEO, Philip Hargrove.

"Afternoon folks. Mr. Hargrove, Ms. Norton, why don't you take chairs in my office, and I'll be right in."

"Chief Friedman," Hargrove said, "I believe we can resolve this quickly."

"Thoroughly is my motto, but that doesn't have to mean long." She smiled. "Sergeant Hammer will offer you coffee."

Hargrove, whose white hair and commanding attitude rarely led anyone to contradict him, frowned, but followed Sergeant Hammer.

No one was in the public area, so Elizabeth gestured Mahan toward the far side of the bullpen. She didn't want to talk in the hallway near her office. "What did you learn?"

He lowered his voice. "Not sure there's much to learn. She didn't see Skelly inject him with anything. The other nurse, Werner, had left. I have her cell number."

"So what's Norton's story?"

Mahan pulled out his thin notebook. "She said she attended Dingle for more than an hour, monitoring his vitals, talking to him so he could wake up more. He asked for ginger ale and toast. She went over to this small kitchenette to get the drink, and put bread in the toaster. She asked another nurse who was on a coffee break if she'd bring the cooked toast back to her."

"Did Norton say that was common practice?"

"Usually they all do their own thing, but the nurse knew she had Dingle, so she said she would."

Elizabeth frowned. "Why did that matter?"

Mahan grimaced. "A number of years ago he had a hernia repair and wrote a strong complaint about the Recovery Room staff. No basis for it, according to Norton. But they wanted to keep him happy."

"And I thought he was just a jerk at work," Elizabeth murmured.

Mahan grinned briefly. "When Norton got back to Dingle's curtained section, Skelly was there. She's not sure Dingle even knew he was around."

"Did they talk?"

"She doesn't think so, but she wasn't there for a minute. Skelly checked the machine that monitors vitals. Norton didn't like that, but she didn't say anything to him about it."

"Did she see Skelly with a syringe in his hand?"

Mahan shook his head. "Nope."

"So, after Skelly left?" Elizabeth asked.

"Just the 'usual stuff' according to Norton. About forty-five minutes later she gave the okay for him to be transferred to his room on the Cardiac Unit."

"How does a syringe figure into this?"

When he was gone, Norton started pitching used supplies, tidying up so housekeeping could clean. She found the used syringe, needle in it, not broken off like when it gets put in the red box."

"Where was it?"

Mahan consulted his notes again." Next to the red sharps box, but on the left side, so it was out of her line of sight. Right about then word came up that Dingle had died."

"But what about the syringe in that location pointed to Skelly?" Elizabeth asked.

"She said she 'put two and two together.' She said, oh here's an interesting part. Dingle dated her mother forty-odd years ago, before her parents were married. When she was little, he sent her birthday cards. When she got older she figured Dingle did it to tick off her father. But she still liked that he sent them."

Elizabeth could not see how two plus two would get to the number four. "So, she seems to have liked Dingle, and she thought by accusing Skelly she was somehow standing up for Dingle?"

Mahan shrugged. "I think she really believes something happened that wasn't natural. Skelly had tried to grab the guy at the council meeting, then he was next to the gurney. She went from there."

"You can't even call that a tenuous link."

"Agreed." He shut his notebook. "There's one more thing. Did you get a close-up look at her?"

Elizabeth frowned. "I stood next to her a couple of times, but I suppose I multi-tasked. At least in my head. What did you see?"

"Really small pupils," Mahan said.

"Damn. Opioid use, you think?"

Mahan waved his hand, palm down. "I know some blood pressure meds my mom was on did that. I'm just suggesting we watch for other signs."

"Great observation. Thanks."

"You, uh, talked to Skelly?" Mahan asked.

She half-smiled. "I told Calderone he was in charge, and he threw me out of the conference room."

CHAPTER FIVE

NORMA NORTON AND PHILIP HARGROVE sat motionless, not looking at each other, as Elizabeth entered her office. In a firm tone, she said, "Good afternoon."

Before she sat behind her desk, Hargrove said, "Chief, I think we can resolve this right now. Dr. Hutton is an esteemed member of the medical..."

Elizabeth held up a hand. Hargrove stopped.

"There's an expression you hear a lot since 9-11." When they said nothing, she continued, "When you see something, say something."

Norton whispered, "I may have spoken too quickly."

Hargrove tried again, "We expect some reflection, some judgment."

Elizabeth smiled tightly. "True. But how many times have you heard an anguished interview with, say, a teacher or ER staffer after a child dies? They felt they should have said something earlier, but didn't want to speak because they weren't positive a broken arm came from abuse."

Hargrove stiffened.

Elizabeth turned to Norton and looked directly into her hazel eyes with their pinpoint pupils. "Mahan gave me details on his conversation with you. I understand how unnatural it was to find an extra syringe in such a carefully planned space. Was there something specific that led you to Dr. Hutton?"

"It wasn't just that he was the only unauthorized person there..." When Elizabeth's eyebrows went up, she continued, "in the sense that it's not part of his regular duties to be in the Recovery Room. He works in the ER or, you know, downstairs."

"Right. Did someone ask him to leave?"

Norton's tone hardened. "No one would ever ask a *doctor* to vacate a room."

Hargrove frowned but didn't look at Norton.

Elizabeth smiled. "I get it. Anything else?"

She nodded. "That business at the Council meeting."

"Sure. But anything that you saw in the Recovery Room?"

Norton lowered her eyes. "No, Chief."

Elizabeth met Hargrove's gaze. "I understand why Ms. Norton raised this issue, but it's hard for me to see a link between the syringe and Dr. Hutton." When Hargrove started to interrupt, she added, "Officer Calderone has the lead on some portions of any investigation we may do. He could see things differently, but I'd be surprised."

Hargrove sat up straighter. "You think Mr. Dingle's death was from something other than natural causes?"

"That's not up to me to decide. As a lay person, I don't see anything unusual, but my guess is you'll have an independent pathologist examine him thoroughly."

Hargrove's face darkened. "They'll have to now."

Elizabeth looked to Norton. "I'm not your boss, but tell me how you think you should have handled this differently."

She sighed. "I should have kept my mouth shut."

"Not necessarily. Maybe report it to someone above you before you publicly accuse anyone." Elizabeth said this as gently as she could, given how angry she felt. In a small town, Skelly's reputation might not survive being called the murderer of a senior city official. No matter how vile the person.

"Where is Dr. Hutton?" Hargrove asked.

Elizabeth stood. "I'll let him know to contact you." She didn't want hospital personnel matters hashed out in the police station.

Hargrove and Norton stood as he spoke. "I understand you have one of our boxes of used syringes. I'd like that back."

"Not yet," Elizabeth said.

He leaned forward an inch or so. "That's hospital property."

Elizabeth kept her expression impassive. "I may want to have prints identified." She nodded at Norton. "Maybe someone missed the box accidentally, maybe not." She looked back to Hargrove. "If the cause of death is natural I'll have the box returned immediately."

Hargrove's goodbye was not even perfunctorily polite. Norton started to say something, but changed her mind and followed him out.

Elizabeth sat in her chair and leaned her back and neck against it. Every inch of her spine felt tight.

Hammer poked his head into her office. "Skelly off the hook?"

"Pretty sure. Is he still down with Calderone?"

"Yeah. What was that woman thinking?"

"She was reacting, not thinking. Mahan here?" When Hammer nodded, she said, "Have him come to the conference room. You're welcome to join us."

"Working on that vacancy announcement you wanted. Tony'll fill me in."

Elizabeth stood, rubbing her neck. "Grab three waters from the fridge in the break room, would you?"

Hammer returned before Elizabeth had picked up her notebook. She took the water and made her way down the hall to the conference room.

She started to enter, but instead knocked with one of the bottles. "May I come in?"

"At your own risk," Skelly called.

"Yes, Chief," said Calderone.

Elizabeth went in and kicked the door shut with her heel. She tossed a bottle of water to each man. "It's over, I think."

Skelly opened his bottle and drained half of it. "You're sure?"

"What the hell was she thinking?" Calderone asked.

Elizabeth pointed at Skelly with her unopened bottle. "As sure as anyone can be." To Calderone she said, "She wasn't. Dingle sent her birthday cards as a child. She heard he died and reacted with emotion, maybe even grief."

Skelly stood and began to pace the room on his side of the conference table. "And I'm supposed to feel sorry for her or something?"

"I didn't say that. My guess is that if she doesn't lose her job she gets demoted or put on some kind of unpaid leave. Hargrove was furious."

"Hargrove?" Skelly asked.

"He came over with her. Angry at her, not you."

Skelly sat down.

Calderone looked from him to Elizabeth. "How do we write this up?"

She shrugged. "My instinct is as a false accusation, with a note that the accuser believed herself for half-an-hour."

"She's a good nurse," Skelly said.

"Who made a very bad decision, for which I expect you'll get a full apology. Hargrove asked if you were here. I told him I'd let you know he asked."

Skelly grimaced. "Hell, I don't even know if I'm allowed on hospital property."

Elizabeth grinned. "Maybe stay out of autopsy until somebody else finishes with Dingle."

The conference room door opened. Mahan said, "Dr. Prasad wants to know if he can talk to Skelly."

"Where's the call?" Elizabeth asked.

Mahan nodded toward the office phone, on a credenza behind the conference table. "Flashing light."

Skelly walked around the table to talk to Prasad.

Calderone looked at Elizabeth. "Sorry about ordering you around."

"By the book. Would have looked very bad if I conducted an interview." She grinned. "No demerits."

"Whew." He tilted his neck from side to side. "Tense."

In a lower voice, Elizabeth said, "In a few minutes, talk to Mahan about something he noted about the nurse who accused Skelly."

Calderone nodded, without changing his expression.

Skelly hung up the phone. "Hey."

They craned their heads toward him.

"Initial bloodwork evaluation indicated someone may have injected some alcohol into Dingle's bloodstream."

"Like the kind you use in hospitals?" Calderone asked.

"Like maybe vodka." Skelly leaned his tailbone against the credenza.

"Which you drink," Elizabeth said.

Mahan whistled and Calderone said, "Damn."

Skelly held Elizabeth's gaze for a moment before he began to walk around the conference table to sit across from Calderone again. "Prasad called the pathologist from Carlinville. She's already on her way."

Elizabeth frowned. "How long is vodka in a person's system before it kills them? And why does Prasad think it was injected?"

Skelly half-shrugged. "Depends on a lot of things, like the patient's general health, whether someone put it directly in a vein or injected it into, say, arm tissue." He rubbed his left temple for a moment. "Prasad said the blood alcohol content of Dingle's blood was so high that he couldn't have simply drunk it."

"Why not?" Calderone asked.

"Prasad said Dingle wouldn't have been able to carry on a conversation with the mayor. Or anyone else for that matter. Or stand up."

Mahan nodded. "I heard he was arguing with her in her office. Guess he would have had to make sense."

"As much as he ever did." Elizabeth glanced at Skelly. "Those were fast results."

"Just the initial blood draw after someone dies. There'll be a full toxicology work-up."

"Which takes weeks," Calderone said.

Elizabeth looked at Calderone and Mahan. "What kind of murder weapon is vodka?"

"Had to be a convenient one for somebody," Calderone said.

"What do you mean?" Skelly asked.

"It means," Elizabeth said, "That Dingle's murder couldn't have been planned in advance. Whoever did it saw an opportunity and couldn't go into a hospital with obvious weapons."

"Had to be someone he worked with, didn't it?" Mahan asked.

Elizabeth nodded. "A fair guess, but he ticked off a lot of people. We need to start a list of who could have been angry with Mr. Dingle."

Mahan raised his eyebrows and Calderone snorted.

"I know, I know," she said. "Start with admin staff who worked with Dingle. Talk to Carol Maitlin, she's the more senior of the two in his office. See if there were any nasty letters or threatening phone calls. I'm not talking about someone complaining about street cleaning or something, unless they were exceptionally rude."

Skelly stood. "I'll get back to the hospital and find Hargrove. I'd like to call the mayor and ask her what the hell she was thinking when she marched down to autopsy with Norton, but that's probably not a good idea."

"Probably not," Elizabeth said. "I'm about to call her. I'll find a way to ask that."

Back in her office, Elizabeth flipped through phone messages Hammer had left on her desk. One was from Jerry Pew. She put his message on the top of the pile, but called the mayor before Jerry.

While she waited for Maitlin to put her through, Elizabeth pondered the mayor's behavior. She was upset after Dingle collapsed in front of her. Elizabeth didn't know how Norton had presented her opinion to Humphrey. Maybe she made it sound as if she saw Skelly insert a needle into Dingle's arm or IV.

No matter what Humphrey had heard or how upset she was, what ticked off Elizabeth was that the mayor had marched to Skelly's office without calling Elizabeth. She realized she didn't know when Humphrey had secured Calderone to walk with her. She should have asked Calderone.

Humphrey came on the line. "Chief Friedman?"

Elizabeth picked up on the terminology. In private, Humphrey usually called her Elizabeth. "Yes, Mayor. I said I'd report what we found."

"You investigated, personally?"

"I assigned Officer Calderone to question Dr. Hutton. I met with the hospital CEO, Philip Hargrove, who brought Norma Norton to the station."

Humphrey said nothing.

"Norton found a syringe next to the box of used ones, but she saw nothing, *at all*, to indicate Dr. Hutton had touched it, much less used it to inject something into Donald Dingle."

Humphrey spoke quietly. "I see."

"That said, I have the box of syringes. I think you heard the nurse say someone cleaned up the area. I'm going to hold onto the box until we know more."

Humphrey's voice grew stronger. "Who will say how he died?"

"The hospital is having an outside pathologist do so. I understand the person will arrive soon. Now, I have two questions for you. "First, before Dingle collapsed in your office, was he behaving normally?"

Humphrey seemed to catch herself mid snort. "If by normally you mean was he implying he knew more than I did about city business, yes."

"No slurred speech or anything?" Elizabeth asked.

"Nothing like that. What are…?"

"Just covering bases. At the hospital, what did Norton say to you that made you so certain Dr. Hutton had harmed Donald Dingle?"

"After they took him…away, I sat in the waiting room near there, and then I took the elevator to the lobby. Nurse Norton got off the elevator next to mine at the same time. She was looking around kind of wildly and seemed upset, so I asked her what was wrong."

"And she said...?" Elizabeth asked.

"She said Skelly, that's what she called him, had killed Donald Dingle. And she had proof."

"Quietly?" Elizabeth asked.

"Oh, no. I mean, there weren't a lot of people around. While I talked to her, I think the receptionist in the lobby must have called someone. I heard footsteps running down the steps, you know, they're next to the elevator, and Officer Calderone came running out of the stairwell."

Something occurred to Elizabeth. "No one called hospital security?"

"Not that I know of."

"And then the three of you went downstairs, to the medical examiner's suite?"

"Yes. And Elizabeth, I'm sorry."

"I'm sorry, too. I'm going to call Randall Watson in hospital security. If there was evidence, it's been cleaned. But he may find something on security cameras."

Humphrey sighed. "I need to make this up to Skelly. What does he drink?"

"I'm not sure alcohol would be his gift preference at the moment."

CHAPTER SIX

ELIZABETH BEGAN TO MAKE LISTS. The obvious one included people Donald Dingle had angered. No way would it be complete. Still, she was surprised at the number of people she could include without doing any research.

Dingle had fought with Mayor Humphrey countless times, and he made snide comments even in public meetings. If the glass ceiling reflected promotion bias over time, Dingle's behavior toward women in the workplace was the best example of misogyny Elizabeth had personally witnessed.

The mayor had been with him during two key points during Dingle's last, very bad, day – when he collapsed in her office and when she visited his hospital room after he had stents put in. The bottom line, the mayor belonged on the list, however unlikely she had injected vodka into her city clerk.

Given the way Dingle had withheld money from the health center, the three people who testified at the budget hearing would probably lead a long line of angry citizens.

In City Hall one day, Elizabeth heard Dingle go off on Milton Weeks, director of public works. A pothole had damaged the rim of Dingle's car's wheel. Weeks had simply stood there and let Dingle rant.

Final Operation

Elizabeth paused. Maybe the way to handle this was to give several officers the task of compiling lists independently. Then they could meet to go over them. She buzzed Hammer and relayed the instruction.

They could come up with a long list, but Elizabeth assumed Dingle's apparent murder was largely a crime of opportunity. His visit to the hospital had not been planned, and how many people carried a flask of vodka with them?

They wouldn't have needed anything that big. Just a single-serving, plastic bottle from a drug or convenience store.

The thought gave her pause. If the local radio station mentioned an ambulance transported someone from City Hall to the hospital, hundreds of people could have known Dingle was in the hospital within a few minutes of his arrival.

His killer didn't have to be someone who planned the killing in advance, just someone who had reason to be in the hospital – whether a legitimate or created reason. Or knew someone who was already there. A nursing assistant or even cafeteria worker could have gotten a call and managed to get near Dingle. Anyone carrying flowers would look like they were visiting a patient.

But people who worked in hospitals were there to save lives. *Not everyone might be dedicated to saving Dingle.* "Not funny," she said aloud.

Dingle would have had people around him most of the time, but he wasn't under guard. The hospital had security cameras in many locations, though she thought not too many in treatment areas. How easy would it have been to go into his ER cubicle, or even to the room he went to after surgery?

As she bent over her list again, Hammer buzzed to tell her hospital security was on the phone. She lifted her receiver. "Mr. Watson. We have to stop meeting like this."

"Chief. I agree. I was out of my office when Sergeant Hammer called. I went to look at security footage. It's in that addition at the back of the hospital."

Elizabeth could envision the one-story, brown brick appendage on the south side of the building. It looked as if it had been plopped down and plugged into the hospital. "Was it built for your security equipment?"

"And, in the old days, to be shared with some big computer servers. They're gone, of course, and we have ten video screens that continuously monitor the hospital."

"Did you spot Donald Dingle in many locations?"

"Unfortunately not. We're always juggling patient privacy with keeping an eye on hallways. When he was taken from the ER to the Cath lab he was in view. And from the Recovery Room to the elevator, and from the elevator on the cardiac floor to the beginning of the hallway that led to his room."

"Nothing outside his room?" Elizabeth asked.

"I'm afraid not. On every floor we have a camera pointing next to a window at the end of the hall. We can move it remotely, in case of emergency. But we don't routinely scan the halls. We'd catch the backsides of a lot of patients."

Elizabeth half-chuckled. "I get that. I expect different people pushed his gurney."

Watson seemed to shuffle papers, and his voice grew quiet, then louder again. "Always hospital transport staff. You might sometimes have a nurse or aide move someone from Recovery to a patient room late in the evening or something. Not this time."

"You know the staff who moved him?"

Watson's tone was emphatic. "One person each time. One's been here five years, one nine. I'd trust them to transport my kids."

"Good to know. One of my officers will talk to them, see if anyone approached them to say hello to Mr. Dingle. We'll get their impression of the world around them while they were with him."

"I already alerted them." He rattled off their names and phone numbers.

"Jordon Hicks I think I've met somewhere," Elizabeth said, "Henry Binder I don't think so."

"Jordon's active in community stuff. Lions Club, collects toys for the Mission every Christmas."

"Right. He stops by the station to collect toys or donations."

Final Operation

"Binder's the one who's been here five years. His wife runs a day care center in their home."

Elizabeth nodded to herself. "Then his wife and he would have had to pass background checks."

"He had to pass one for the job here," Watson said.

"Of course. You'll hang onto those tapes, or digital files, in case I need to look at them?"

"Already downloading them. Could be easier to send someone here. I'd be happy to sit with them. Any of us would."

Elizabeth called Calderone's cell phone. "Don't think we'll get much from hospital security video, but Watson said we can stop by. Maybe easier to review them there."

"Dingle on it at all?" he asked.

"Just a couple times in the hallway. The important news is they don't use the cameras to look for hospital gowns that aren't tied tight."

"Good to know. I'll swing by there first thing tomorrow. I can look at the times before and after he's on camera. Unless you want me to go tonight."

"If he'd been on camera much, I'd say go now, but I don't think the video will show much. We'll talk to the men who escorted him on gurneys."

Elizabeth hung up and leaned back in her chair. She wished she could put an ad in the paper or a question on Facebook to ask who despised Donald..."Damn!"

She picked up the phone and called Jerry Pew. After five-thirty. Maybe she'd get lucky and he'd be at some local event chowing down the free food. No such luck.

"Chief? Been expecting you'd call me back. I been hearing all kinds of rumors. I'm hoping the least likely one is that a doctor put one of those stent things in upside down."

Elizabeth had to smile. "Only a rumor. Not a lot known yet. My understanding is that a pathologist is coming from another hospital to do the autopsy."

"Well, that gets to my main question. Did Skelly really kill our beloved city clerk?"

"I thought newspaper editors weren't supposed to jump to conclusions."

Jerry chuckled. "It's not funny. But we all know what a bas...jerk the guy was. Folks sayin' you brought Skelly to the station for questioning."

Elizabeth hesitated. "I think the hospital might clarify for you, but I'll..."

"Hospital basically told me to go to hell." He chuckled again. "Could meet Dingle."

"Jerry!"

"Oh, I'm just joshin'. I talked to Donald Dingle five times a week, seems like. Hard to think of him as dead."

Hammer walked in and handed her a note. *Dr. Prasad on hold.*

To Hammer, Elizabeth said, "I'll take it in one minutes." He left.

"Listen, Jerry, I have an important call. Best way to put it is that someone at the hospital made a hasty allegation. After thinking about it, they apologized and withdrew it."

"Pretty loud allegation," Jerry said.

"So I've heard. Why don't you call Skelly? I have to go." Elizabeth hung up and pushed the blinking light on her phone. "Dr. Prasad?"

"Yes, chief. I have a question. Probably ten."

"I'll do my best."

"Since Dr. Hutton was in the police station when I talked to him, I'm sure you heard initial bloodwork identified vodka in Mr. Dingle's system. Far more than a person could drink and function even minimally."

"He relayed some of what you said."

"So, the pathologist from Carlinville is here. It's not normal for me to...participate to the degree that I am in assisting her, but the chief medical officer and Mr. Hargrove asked me to be available for Dr. Curran. That's the pathologist from Carlinville."

"Because you were Mr. Dingle's surgeon today?"

"And because I was in the autopsy suite when Dr. Hutton was…removed. I remained in the suite so there would be no question of anyone else being near the body."

"You did hear Nurse Norton has acknowledged that she saw nothing to implicate Dr. Hutton?"

"Yes." He sighed. "Mr. Hargrove came down. So…unnecessary."

"I think she thought she was doing the right thing at the time," Elizabeth said.

"Be that as it may, my question is this. When Dr. Curran finishes her work this evening – it will be quite late – what do I do? Do I call you? Call security to lock up the suite?"

"I can answer part of that, or at least start the answer. I'm sure Dr. Curran knows the process for preserving the body."

"What else is there?"

"She'll head home. It will be a day, at least, before she completes her initial report."

Dr. Prasad sighed. "She said that. And she won't have full toxicology information for weeks."

"She'll provide her report to me and the state's attorney," Elizabeth said. "Do you know Xavier Donaldson?"

"Just from the papers."

"My officers and I investigate the crime, but Mr. Donaldson gives the police and medical examiner his guidance on things such as preserving evidence, when to release a body to next of kin. I'll ask him to call you."

"I have a message from his secretary to call him. I didn't know if that would be stepping on your toes."

Elizabeth smiled to herself. Donaldson was the biggest stuffed shirt in town. Dr. Prasad didn't need to know she thought that. "We work closely together. Go ahead and return the call."

"Long day," Prasad said.

An idea came to Elizabeth. "Did you get anything to eat?"

"This place is not conducive to food, Chief."

"It is not. You need to eat. How about I bring several kinds of subs over? You and Dr. Curran can do more on full stomachs."

When he agreed, Elizabeth hung up, glad she'd found a way to possibly get more information on Dingle's cause of death.

AT SIX-THIRTY, ELIZABETH PULLED into the hospital parking lot with a bag containing six half-sub sandwiches. She also had a liter of cola and several cups the sub shop provided. In a hospital she could always find ice.

Contrary to his concerns about eating in the autopsy suite, Dr. Prasad polished off a tuna salad sub and a veggie one. Dr. Curran said she could use a break and joined them in the outer office. Thankfully, from Elizabeth's perspective, minus the apron she wore as she worked.

A short woman, Fiona Curran's lips were as thin as the rest of her. She did have a friendly demeanor. She reached for a chicken salad sub. "I wasn't born yesterday, Chief Friedman. I know you're fishing for information."

Elizabeth smiled briefly. "While I wouldn't mind any, the subs require no payment, monetary or otherwise."

"Not much to tell. My guess is injected vodka killed him, but I have a lot of work to do before I issue a finding." Curran nodded in Dr. Prasad's direction. "If I know someone who needs a stent put in, I can recommend Dr. Prasad's work."

"That's reassuring, I suppose," he said.

Elizabeth picked up a cold cut sub. "Your report will tell us a lot. I guess my biggest question is whether the vodka had to be given to him in the hospital, or whether it could have been inserted before he arrived."

Curran gave an exaggerated shrug. "You can't hold me to this yet, but I would think it had to be relatively soon before he died. Your body absorbs alcohol more slowly when you drink it. Your liver plays the biggest role in getting it out of your bloodstream, and it takes time to work."

Elizabeth nodded slowly. "I have charts on how quickly people absorb alcohol they drink based on varying weights. But nothing on putting it directly into a vein."

"Do we even know it went into a vein?" Prasad asked. "Could it have been delivered intramuscularly?"

Final Operation

"I'm examining him for needle punctures where we don't expect to find any," Curran said, "but my guess at this point would be via a vein. Not only did Dingle have an IV port in place, hospitals do many blood draws on heart attack patients. Why not put in a fluid rather than draw one out?"

"So, probably here, then?" Elizabeth asked.

Curran nodded. "I repeat, don't repeat what I say. Maybe he didn't get the stuff within a few minutes, but I'd be surprised if it was as much as an hour. I'm trying to determine whether it was administered through his IV. If I can tell that, it gives you law enforcement types what I believe you call a more narrow window."

Prasad frowned. "So I wouldn't likely have smelled something during surgery?"

Curran shook her head. "Even if he'd been injected before you worked on him, maybe not. Vodka has little odor, and there are lots of operating room smells, some of them similar to pure ethyl alcohol. Heck, every time I'm in an operating room it's so cold my nose runs. Does yours?"

Prasad smiled. "No, but that happens to a couple nurses who work with me."

Elizabeth balled up a sub wrapper. "Bottom line, I need to map out every minute of Dingle's time from not long before he collapsed in the mayor's office to when he died. And who was near him."

"In the old days," Prasad said, "people went to cardiac ICU after stent placement. Then we'd have a better idea of who was with him."

"That hospital is a busy place," Elizabeth said. "The cardiac floor where he died was quiet, but he was also in the ER, maybe radiology, the Cardiac Cath Lab, elevators, hallways. Even though he was on a stretcher, lots of people could have come up to him."

"With a needle?" Prasad asked.

"If you had it ready to use," Curran said, "you'd only need a few seconds."

CHAPTER SEVEN

ELIZABETH'S BACK ACHED, likely from the day's tension, as she trudged up the external stairway to the privacy of her two-bedroom apartment in Edna Schmidt's Victorian house. Usually she found it almost too quiet. At seven-thirty after the day she'd just had, Elizabeth welcomed the silence.

A streak of orange and brown hurled toward her from its hiding place under the couch, and she accepted the cat's head-butting as her due for working late. "Okay, okay. I'll have food in your bowl in two shakes."

Lucky meowed loudly and shoved her head into Elizabeth's calf, trying to guide her to the kitchen. Elizabeth followed her directions and filled a bowl with dry food. She placed a few soft treats on the floor next to the bowl. Lucky wolfed them down and then had her head over the dry food in three seconds.

After Elizabeth drank a tall glass of orange juice, she called Skelly. "You doing okay?"

"Sitting here stewing. I don't know what the mayor was thinking, bringing the nurse to the suite without calling security, or you. Could have been ironed out in a two-minute conversation."

Elizabeth turned on a burner under her kettle. "A very poor decision. I guess she was upset and thought she was supposed to do something."

Skelly blew out air. "I suppose if I asked you to meet me at the Weed 'n Feed for a beer people would say you were hanging out with a felon fellow."

Elizabeth smiled. "They would then accuse me of bias if I didn't suggest the state's attorney...hey. Donaldson never even called me."

Skelly's voice rose. "You sent him evidence?"

"Nothing to send. When something's going on he usually calls to see if I plan to pull his office into the loop. He didn't."

"Probably figured it was a crock," Skelly said.

Elizabeth jotted a note on a pad she kept in the corner of her kitchen counter. "Maybe. Listen, we were so busy establishing who was where today, I don't think I asked you if you saw anything unusual."

"Like what?"

"Like anyone in the Recovery Room or ER you didn't know?

Skelly said nothing for a few seconds. "I don't think so. I don't know everyone by name, but I recognized the staff I saw. The few people in the ER who weren't staff seemed to clearly be with patients."

"What about beyond that? Anyone standing in hallways near where Dingle was?"

"Not that I recall. Certainly not someone holding up a syringe and a bottle of vodka."

Elizabeth pulled a teabag from a jar on the counter. "Funny."

"I wasn't trying to be funny. If it was in the evening, someone roaming the halls might stand out, but not during the day. Always lots of people around."

"OK. On another topic, I guess Dr. Curran will finish her work pretty soon."

"She's close to done," Skelly said. "I had a call from Philip Hargrove a few minutes ago. He said she'll leave some notes on my desk and we should have the preliminary report in a day or so. He wants me to call her if I have any questions."

"Does he usually give instructions to the medical staff?" Elizabeth asked.

"He said he talked to the chief medical officer. My guess is Hargrove called me because Dr. Roman wants to keep out of it. He'll probably have to talk to the chief nurse about Norton's accusation."

"Did he talk to you about it?"

"Dr. Roman, no. I already told Hargrove I didn't think he should fire her."

"What did he say?"

"I forget his exact words, but they boiled down to he was in charge of personnel matters."

"He is pretty formal." When Skelly didn't reply, Elizabeth continued, "I should be too busy for breakfast or lunch tomorrow, but how about dinner at the diner?"

"Sounds good. See you about seven."

After they said good-bye, Elizabeth poured a cup of tea and glanced at her foot where a more contented Lucky had placed a paw. "You're welcome. Don't make me spill hot tea on you."

WEDNESDAY MORNING, ELIZABETH took extra care with her uniform and got to the office at seven-thirty. She studied the police blotter from the day before and decided the only important thing she missed when busy with Dingle's death was another car break-in at the college. "That's odd."

She walked to the break room and poured water into the coffee pot reservoir and added a filter and coffee before she turned on the pot. Hammer made it too strong for her taste, so she never minded being the one to start the first pot.

The back door to the station opened and Hammer called, "I smell coffee. That you, Chief?"

"Yep. Perfect timing."

He came to the doorway. "Uh, what did you think of Jerry Pew's article?"

Elizabeth groaned. "I must be the last place on the paperboy's route. How bad is it?"

Final Operation

Hammer took the paper from under his arm and handed it to her. "He implied Skelly was off the hook, then he says maybe he isn't. But it's almost worse than that. Makes it sound as if every patient is in danger."

"Great." Elizabeth placed her as-yet unfilled coffee cup next to the coffee maker and reviewed the story."

Hospital Murder Has
Town Up in Arms

The murder of City Clerk Donald Dingle at Logland Memorial Hospital on Tuesday shocked the town. Dingle had a heart attack at City Hall at about eight-thirty A.M., during an argument with the mayor. He had what seemed to be successful surgery to implant stents, but died after being transported to his private room on the Cardiac Unit.

Autopsy results were not available for this morning's edition of the Logland Press. The hospital refused to offer any explanation for Dingle's death, but an unnamed individual (who was not authorized to speak on the matter) indicated that Dingle may have been injected with a foreign substance.

There was initially speculation that a hospital staff member had been responsible for such an action, but this was later strongly refuted by hospital CEO Philip Hargrove. Because the allegation appears to have been unfounded, the Logland Press is not naming the individual who was mistakenly accused. The Press will continue to pursue information on why the accusation was made.

Elizabeth glanced at Hammer. "Jerry's not naming Skelly because he likes to get information from him for stories."

He nodded. "Keep reading."

The Logland Police Department, which Dingle has advocated eliminating, plans to work with hospital staff to learn the cause of Dingle's death and whether it was due to natural causes, an accident, or malicious intent on the part of a hospital employee or anyone else.

A local resident visiting family members at the hospital expressed concern. "If they can't say how Mr. Dingle died or who did it, does that mean that no patient is safe?"

A hospital spokesperson did not return a call to respond to the same question. More information will be in Friday's paper, with real-time updates provided on the Logland Press website.

Elizabeth returned the paper to Hammer. "One of Jerry Pew's more irresponsible articles."

Hammer nodded. "At least he didn't say we should have already identified the killer."

"There is that."

Hammer shifted his weight from one foot to the other. "You might also like to take a look at a letter to the editor."

"About…?"

"Need for a police department in Logland." Hammer turned to walk back to his desk.

Elizabeth called after him. "Afraid I'll throw the paper at you?"

Over his shoulder he called, "Or a cup of coffee."

Elizabeth turned to the last interior page of the twelve-page paper. The headline read, "Substantial Savings Possible."

At its Tuesday meeting, the late Donald Dingle, Logland city clerk, raised the possibility of eliminating the Logland Police Department and replacing its staff with patrols by county sheriff deputies. The writer thinks it's about time.

A town the size of Logland doesn't need eight full-time officers. What do eight people do in that station all day? You never see more than two or three of them at a time. And why do eight officers need a full-time chief? Eight people should be able to manage themselves!

The letter listed several recent crimes, and questioned why the city police had not prevented them. It speculated this was because officers stayed in the station counting their salaries.

Finally, the writer said he didn't want his name used because he feared he'd be stopped for speeding even if he (or she) wasn't. The name attached was, "A concerned Logland citizen."

To herself, Elizabeth said, "More like stopping him from being a public nuisance." She walked to her office.

Hammer called from the bullpen. "Who do you think wrote it?"

"Probably Jerry himself. I think he does that to generate responses.

"Not good for morale," Hammer called.

"Ignore it." She glanced down at the report on her desk and raised her voice to ask, "What's with another car break-in at the college?"

"Kind of odd. Someone rifled the glove box, but didn't touch a bunch of expensive CDs. Guess they were looking for cash."

"I'll talk to President Dodd in an hour or so. I'm curious about that briefcase stolen from his car yesterday. When Calderone and Mahan get in, I'd like the four of us to meet."

"Sure thing, Chief."

Elizabeth called the hospital CEO, whose cool hello indicated he was not pleased to hear from her. "Mr. Hargrove, I wanted to let you know we'd be talking to some of your staff over the next couple of…"

"You'll go through me, of course."

"I don't mind letting you know what we're doing, and we'll try not to interfere. We won't be seeking permission, of course."

"You'll be on hospital property," he began.

"As we are on the site of any murder investigation. Unless you want us to bring anyone we choose to question down to the police station. I can arrange that."

Hargrove said nothing for several seconds. "I believe that would be more disruptive."

"If you like, you can designate an interview room for most of the conversations." Elizabeth had planned to offer him that option, but didn't want him to think he would designate who they would talk to, or when.

"That would be fine. There's one just outside my office."

"I'd like something away from the administrative suite. I don't want interviewees to get the impression that management is monitoring who we talk to." *Especially since you probably want them to think that.*

In a formal tone, Hargrove said, "I don't think the training classrooms are in use today. I'll assign you one on the second floor. You'll have to stop by my office for a key."

"Sounds good."

Elizabeth stared at her phone for a few seconds after hanging up. In truth, she didn't yet have a list for hospital staff to talk to. She started to type one.

- Gurney transporters Jordon Hicks and Henry Binder
- Nurse Werner – unless Mahan reached her
- ER physicians and nurses
- Anyone who drew Dingle's blood
- X-Ray staff who might have worked with him
- EKG people
- Recovery Room staff besides Norton and Werner
- Staff who assisted Dr. Prasad in the Cardiac Cath Lab
- EMTs in Dingle's ambulance

Elizabeth's sense of urgency grew with every name or function on the list. These interviews would easily span two days, especially because employees' hospital shifts and workdays varied.

Hammer buzzed her intercom and she picked up. "Chief, Calderone and Mahan are out here. Send them in?"

"Yes, thanks." She printed four copies of the list. Mahan and Calderone would add to it. She'd revise it and give one to Hammer so he could keep track of who they interviewed.

Final Operation

Elizabeth sat at her desk again, but voices in the bullpen distracted her. Hammer sounded frustrated. "Yes ma'am, I get that, but Chief Friedman is up to her eyeballs."

The woman's voice was harder to hear, but when she strained, Elizabeth realized it was Alice from the bookstore. And she sounded very insistent.

Elizabeth stood and walked into the bullpen. A stubborn-looking Alice faced Hammer from the public side of the large counter. She gestured with a book. "This will be a big...oh, good, here you are."

"Alice." Elizabeth smiled at Hammer. "I've got this."

Alice beamed. "I have just the thing, Chief Friedman."

"Elizabeth. What's up, Alice? What's the book?"

"It's called the *Poisoner's Handbook*, and it'll help you figure out what got injected into Donald Dingle." She handed the book across the counter.

Elizabeth opened it to the Table of Contents. Cyanides, arsenic, mercury and, to Elizabeth's surprise, ethyl alcohol. She didn't associate hard liquor with poisoning, though many people essentially poisoned their livers with long-term use. Methyl alcohol, wood alcohol, killed quickly, and was responsible for a lot of deaths and blindness during Prohibition. But ethyl alcohol?

"Thanks, Alice. I'll go through this and return it."

"It's my personal copy. Keep it as long as you like."

"Uh, Alice, why do you have a book on poisoning people?"

Her always-friendly face scowled. "Well, of course, I keep it for information on what could happen, not to plan to kill someone."

"Ah. Of course."

Alice leaned across the counter. "The library has a copy of this book. Anyone could learn how to poison someone." Alice turned, waved over her shoulder, and walked out.

Elizabeth faced Hammer, who had returned to his desk and begun signing supply requisitions. "Good to know we have a poison cookbook."

"And a crazy bookstore owner," he muttered.

"Dr. Curran did think ethyl alcohol killed Dingle."

Hammer stopped writing mid-signature. "You really think that book taught someone what to do?"

Elizabeth grinned. "Not when they could go to the Internet."

She returned to her office and read. Though she learned some of the more graphic aspects of death from hard drinking, the book didn't discuss injecting alcohol. Apparently no one tried that during Prohibition, which the book discussed in detail.

Twenty minutes later, Calderone came in carrying a notepad and coffee, Mahan a yellow legal pad.

"Let's hear who you think we need to interview," Elizabeth said.

They put their lists on her desk and each studied the three lists. Calderone's had only a few at the hospital, and ten at various locations in City Hall. Mahan had fewer at the hospital and half of the city's Public Works Department.

"Why so many in Public Works?" she asked.

"He probably rode them hardest," Mahan said. "Always on them to plow the streets faster or get to every pothole on the first day of good weather. One time Dingle told Weeks in Public Works he didn't give a crap if it was Good Friday, he wanted the yellow lines in the city parking lot repainted because they weren't bright enough."

Elizabeth shook her head. "Any chance the maligned Mr. Weeks was in the mayor's office or at the hospital yesterday?"

Mahan laughed. "Nah."

"But his son is on the hospital paramedic staff," Calderone said. "I don't know if he was in the ER that day."

No one said anything for several seconds, until Elizabeth did. "Just goes to show how interlaced much of this investigation will be." She sat back in her chair. "I'll take first crack at the people in the mayor's and Dingle's immediate offices. Oh, and the budget staff. They worked with him the most, don't you think?"

Mahan shrugged, and Calderone nodded.

Elizabeth thought of something. "Calderone, how did you happen to hear the mayor or Norton shouting in the hospital lobby?"

He snapped his fingers. "Damn. I'd gone over there to look for you. I was walking down from the third floor."

"Why damn?" Elizabeth asked.

"Hammer told me President Dodd wanted you to call him. I plain forgot after that."

Elizabeth waved a hand. "He knows we had our hands full. I'll call him in a few minutes. Did you go by the hospital to look at security cameras yet?"

Calderone shook his head. "Hammer said you wanted to meet."

"Okay. Hargrove is going to give us a key to a training room to do some staff interviews. Mahan can get that going, and I'll head to City Hall." She nodded at Calderone. "After you look at the tapes meet up with Mahan." Her gaze took in both of them. "Try to start interviews by department, rather than scattershot."

"Any particular order?" Mahan asked.

"I don't know. Maybe start with ER and ask them what Dingle's progression was through the hospital. Try to follow that, but you may need to skip around. Depends on people's schedules."

"Don't you figure their bosses would let them come almost any time?" Mahan asked.

Elizabeth shrugged. "They'll be helpful when they can, but if there are only a couple people in X-Ray or someplace, they may not be able to leave. I don't want us roaming the hospital unless we have to. I think the Recovery Room is busiest on weekdays...hey, Mahan."

He looked up from his notebook. "What?"

"The other Recovery Room nurse, Werner. What did she have to say?"

"She put the needle the other nurse, Norton, found in the red sharps box."

"How did she know to clean up Norton's space?"

"Oh, right." He flipped a couple of pages. "She'd been in the ladies room and came back to finish clean-up in her area, when she walked by Norton. Norton was holding a syringe, and Werner joked with her about where to stick it."

"Medical humor," Elizabeth said. "Rarely funny."

Calderone shrugged. "Most nurses don't like cop humor."

"Okay, so Norton had the syringe with a needle," Elizabeth said.

"And she hadn't heard Werner coming, so she was startled. She dropped it on the counter."

"The counter, not the gurney?" Calderone asked.

"Right. Dingle had been taken out on the gurney," Mahan said. "One hadn't replaced it yet."

"So, Norton was near the sharps box on the counter?" Elizabeth asked.

"Not too far. It's a small space, nothing is far from anything. Norton acted excited and told Werner she'd picked it up from the counter. Werner told her she better make sure she hit the box next time, and walked on."

"What? Norton didn't tell Werner she hadn't seen or used the needle previously, or that she didn't know where it came from?"

"Nope. I asked," Mahan said."

Calderone and Elizabeth stared at each other. "She had just used that needle on herself," Calderone said.

"Possibly," Elizabeth said, and Mahan nodded.

"Or on Dingle?" Elizabeth asked.

Calderone shrugged. "He didn't die for what, half an hour? I guess it'll depend on what the autopsy report says. How much vodka got injected and how long he could have tolerated it."

Elizabeth shook her head slowly. "But she had the time to do it and she was alone with him."

Mahan nodded. "If she injected Dingle or herself, why would she make a fuss?"

"To make sure the focus was on someone besides her," Elizabeth said. "Which she had to do once Werner saw her with the syringe."

Calderone aimed his empty coffee cup at Elizabeth's trash can and hit it. "So Skelly's off the hook."

"Looking at Norton in this light makes him even less likely a suspect – not just to our eyes, but anyone else's. But some people will have questions until we arrest the killer."

She pointed to the papers on her desk. "Are we clear on the interviews? You can bet Jerry Pew'll be all over the place, even if it's mostly on the phone. Don't want a story saying we're disrupting everybody."

"Basically, ask what they did with Dingle, who else they saw with him?" Mahan asked.

"And where they got the booze?" Calderone winked.

"Funny," Elizabeth said. "Spend a few minutes to develop some basic questions. Run them by Hammer. Me, too if you want, but until we know more, I think the questions will be pretty standard. I don't need to see them unless you think I do."

She stood. "Okay you two, go make Philip Hargrove's day."

CHAPTER EIGHT

ELIZABETH CALLED PRESIDENT DODD'S office at the college as soon as Calderone and Mahan left. His secretary asked her to hold for two minutes. When Dodd came on the line, he sounded less officious than usual.

"Chief. Difficult time for you. Thank you for returning my call."

"Thanks for understanding. I see that in addition to the car break-ins night before last, there was another last night."

"Yes. But my primary concern is the briefcase removed from my vehicle."

"Which was in front of your university residence?"

Dodd cleared his throat. "Yes. I generally bring it in, but I had a binder of materials for the board meeting later this week. I should have gone back out for the briefcase."

"I noted its contents, which seem to be largely paperwork."

Dodd expelled air as a kind of whoosh. "The problem is, I had files on some senior staff performance reviews. It would be...embarrassing if they were made public."

"To you or the senior staff?" Elizabeth asked.

He hesitated. "Both."

"Okay, we'll be on alert for the briefcase. It would be hard to spot the contents if they're out of the case, unless they were left in plain sight. Are you sure that's all that was in there?"

"I thought of two more items."

Elizabeth waited for him to continue.

Dodd cleared his throat. "One was a memo from the late Donald Dingle."

When Dodd's pause extended to several seconds, Elizabeth said, "And?"

"The memo summarized his proposal that campus security handle activity in the area immediately around the college, not just on campus."

Elizabeth felt herself flush. "That would take a broader mutual cooperation agreement than we now have with you. Did he say why he would ask that?"

"I don't have to tell you he wanted to eliminate your department. His rationale was that much of what crime there is in Logland is on campus or involves students. He thought we should 'pull more of our weight,' as he put it."

"Did you have a chance to discuss the idea with him?" she asked.

"When we talked about it over the phone, I told him I'd have to talk to you, and any extra staff we might hire – which I told him I didn't want to do – would have to be paid for by city funds."

Elizabeth kept herself from laughing. "And what did he say to that?"

"Nothing I care to repeat. What did he have against you anyway?"

Elizabeth shrugged, then realized Dodd could not see her. "I think because I haven't been here forever he couldn't get me under his thumb. He wanted everyone to be in his debt."

"Makes sense. Anyway, I told him to send me a memo or proposal in writing. It was hand-delivered day before yesterday. I planned to read it that night."

"Was it from only him?" she asked.

"That's all I remember. The mayor was not on the from line, nor was she copied."

I bet she wasn't. "Was anyone else?"

"He copied one council member. The one who agrees with him all the time."

"Adrian Gangle," Elizabeth said. "So you didn't read it?"

"I didn't. After the briefcase disappeared, I asked my secretary if she read it. She said she opened the envelope, but it was folded and marked to be read only by me. So, she didn't read or photocopy it."

"If it becomes relevant, I can probably find a copy at City Hall. Now, you said you had one other item?"

"Did you know I'm a type one diabetic?"

That took Elizabeth by surprise. It was his business, but she went to various meetings with the college president. If he were to collapse, it would be good to know he had diabetes. "No. I'm assuming you control it well."

"I'm rigorous in managing my condition. I did, uh, have two doses of insulin in the briefcase."

"That's not medication anyone would misuse is it?" she asked.

"It's labeled, so no one but an addict would even think of injecting it."

Needles, of course. "You're concerned as much about the syringes as the medicine."

"Yes. Your officers have worked with campus security on needle safety, and here I go and make two syringes available."

"Did anyone besides you know what was in your briefcase?" Elizabeth asked.

"My wife and a couple staff know about the insulin. Only my secretary knew the performance reviews were in there."

"I know Sergeant Hammer has talked to your security folks. Do you have a photo of the briefcase?"

"It wouldn't help. Brown, boxy, no special markings. There's a more detailed description in the police report I filed."

"I'll check it out," she said.

Dodd cleared his throat again. "I do hope you won't be forced to open the briefcase. It is locked."

Elizabeth thought about that for a moment. "Unless it's smoking, I see no need. As long as I can be sure it's yours."

His irritation came through clearly. "How many other stolen brown briefcases were reported lately?"

Elizabeth hung up, thinking that if Dingle went so far as to talk to Dodd, he was an even bigger SOB than she'd thought. She wondered if the mayor had any idea how much Dingle, and it appeared Gangle, had done behind her back.

She buzzed Hammer to let him know what Dodd had said. "Did Dodd talk to you about much?"

"He said he'd filed a report but 'wanted a word' with you."

Elizabeth told him about the insulin. "I'd like you to mention the medicine to the others, but his medical condition is private. I'm only telling you because of the syringes." She didn't mention Dingle's memo. For now, she didn't want it to be a topic of discussion.

ELIZABETH DECIDED NOT TO CALL before going to City Hall. Keeping people off balance could be a good thing.

She gaped in surprise when she opened the door to the grouping of offices that housed the mayor, city clerk, budget director, and city treasurer. Outside Dingle's office sat a custodian's wheeled cart with a trashcan, mop, and cleaning supplies. A pile of white storage boxes, still flattened, leaned against the wall near the cart.

From inside Dingle's office, the mayor and Budget Director Patricia Franz seemed to be arguing in low tones. The two secretaries in the outer office in which Elizabeth stood barely looked up. Both seemed to want to concentrate on what they were typing.

Elizabeth glanced from one to the other and cleared her throat. She gestured to Dingle's office. "I'm going to join that party."

The older of the two women, Carol Maitlin, said, "Please do."

Twenty-something Harmony Wilson added, "They need a referee."

Maitlin cleared her throat in seeming disapproval of Wilson's remark.

Elizabeth knocked on the office's door jamb and Humphrey and Franz faced her, both registering surprise at her appearance.

"Looks as if I got here just in time. Were you two about to have Donald Dingle's office cleaned?"

Franz flushed. Against her blonde hair, the reddening almost glowed. "I thought it would help us get over yesterday's bad memories."

Humphrey leaned against Dingle's huge faux-mahogany desk. "While I'd like to erase them, I didn't think you would want the office disturbed until you went through it."

Elizabeth focused on Franz. "You thought right, Madam Mayor. Ms. Franz, what possessed you to tamper with potential evidence?"

Franz's mouth formed an oval, and then she closed it. "I guess it didn't occur to me to think about it that way."

Elizabeth nodded toward the custodian cart. "Has anything been cleaned or removed?"

Both women said no.

Elizabeth gestured toward the door and half-bowed. "I'll let you step out. I should have ordered the office sealed yesterday afternoon, when it appeared he didn't die of natural causes."

"Are you going to go through it now?" Humphrey asked.

"Probably just a cursory look at his desk and inbox, then seal the office in case we need to do more later. I'd like to spend most of my time today talking to folks in the immediate office. Mahan's talking to a few folks in Public Works, but I want to talk to Milton Weeks myself."

"Why?" Franz asked.

"I'll let you know." Elizabeth smiled at them as she shut the office door. She ran her hands threw her chin-length hair. *I focused too much on proving Skelly innocent. I should have thought about protecting the contents of Dingle's office.*

She walked to the window and looked at the parking lot behind City Hall. *What was Franz trying to hide?* Elizabeth felt foolish not to have had Dingle's office sealed. Because the crime had seemingly taken place at the hospital, she hadn't focused on City Hall.

Maybe you were thinking too much about Skelly and not enough about your job.

She turned from the window to take in the room. She'd never been in there unless Dingle was, and he was such a presence a person tended to focus on him not the room. It held little furniture – just his desk and chair, two padded arm chairs across from it, and a small table with four chairs in one corner. A credenza to the right of the desk appeared to also be a lateral file cabinet.

No bookshelves. That seemed odd to Elizabeth, but she could also imagine the imperial Dingle demanding that most items he wanted to study be brought to him only when he wanted them.

Then her eyes took in a large indentation on the carpet, to the left of Dingle's desk. Just the size of a set of bookshelves. Elizabeth felt herself flush. She removed her police blazer and placed it on the back of Dingle's chair and took a pair of latex gloves from her pants pocket.

She crossed the room, opened the door, and spoke to Carol Maitlin when the woman met her gaze. "Who removed shelves from Mr. Dingle's office, and how recently was that done?"

Maitlin nodded as if she'd expected the question. "I believe Ms. Franz did it last night. The budget files had already been moved to the budget office when I got in this morning."

Elizabeth nodded and walked to Franz's office and entered through the open door without knocking.

Franz looked up from a spreadsheet that lay on her desk. "Can I help you, Chief?"

Elizabeth shut the door behind her. "You can tell me what the hell you think you're doing." She thought Franz's frown was a deliberate attempt to look innocent.

"I don't know what you mean."

"You removed those bookshelves from the clerk's office. What else did you tamper with?"

Franz stood and nearly shouted. "Those are my budget binders! He wanted them near him so I had to ask permission to see my own materials."

"Donald Dingle was a controlling person who insulted people who worked around him. But it doesn't give you the right to go into a dead man's office and take items. I repeat, what else did you remove?"

She sat down, frown deepening, and shrugged. "Okay. He kept a folder of what he called 'truth letters' he wrote. I took mine out of a folder in his file cabinet." When Elizabeth simply stared at her, she added, "None of what he said was true!"

Elizabeth kept staring at the woman until Franz dropped her gaze. "I'll need that entire folder, including your letter."

She lifted her chin. "It's still in the drawer. I only took out my letter. And I shredded it."

"In the office shredder?" Elizabeth asked.

Franz's shoulders sagged. "Yes."

Elizabeth gestured to the door. "Show me the shredder, and be prepared to indicate if you think your letter is the top item."

Franz stood, walked around her desk, and entered the reception area. "Carol, did you notice whether anyone used the shredder after I did?" She pointed to a corner of the room, at a shredder that sat atop a thirteen-gallon plastic trash can.

The secretary looked up from stack of papers. "I don't think so."

Before Franz could reply, Elizabeth said, "Good. Ms. Maitlin, could you give me a manila folder? We need to reassemble some materials Ms. Franz shredded."

"Certainly." Maitlin reached into a bottom drawer and pulled out two folders. Her small smile made Elizabeth think Maitlin enjoyed seeing Franz being chastised. Maybe Franz was usually the one to dish it out.

Elizabeth took the folders. "Ms. Franz, you'll want to extract the shredded matter carefully. You'll be taping it back together." She walked to the shredder with Franz and watched the woman pull out a row of shredded paper the width and length of an 8.5 by 11 inch piece of paper.

Final Operation

Franz sat at the corner table in Dingle's office while Elizabeth went through his desk. He did indeed have a 'truth folder' – behind all others in the bottom drawer of his desk – with discipline letters sent to employees. A large folder.

She mentally groaned as she went through Dingle's missives. Four went to the seemingly long-suffering Milton Weeks in Public Works, two to staff in the budget officer, including the one to Franz herself. From Elizabeth's point of view, all the items in Weeks' letters were beyond his control. The city ran out of road salt because of a shortage in the Midwest, and he didn't create the potholes or trample fences in a city park.

A cursory review of the budget-related letters showed they were for things another manger would have simply called to a staff member's attention. A spreadsheet minus the summary page, several pages upside down in Councilman Gangle's budget binder. Elizabeth smiled. *That might be deliberate.*

Franz had not realized Dingle had a duplicate of the letter to her. A draft anyway. He had made a couple handwritten notes in the margin, and had folded the draft in half and placed it in the back of the folder.

The letter was almost malicious. Dingle complained that new spreadsheet software didn't work as he wanted it to, and Franz should have trained him better. Elizabeth figured the student was the problem. Then he went on to criticize how she supervised her staff and said the times she was late because of a sick child were "a situation she should have allowed for."

Elizabeth raised her eyes and met Franz's. "He thought your kid shouldn't get sick?"

She shook her head. "He said I should have had immediate back-up childcare plans."

Elizabeth flipped to another page in the folder as she held Franz's gaze. "Did he have any kids?"

She snorted. "Who would marry him?"

Not Norma Norton's mother. "An open question, I'm sure. How is the taping going?"

"Slowly. Wait, how did you know about my sick son?"

Elizabeth stood with the draft of the letter and walked to her. "He kept a draft. Is this it?"

Franz pursed her lips as she took the copy. "That's it."

"Keep the scraps together and give me the folder, but you don't have to finish the taping."

Her shoulders relaxed. "I'm sorry I shredded it."

"If it makes you feel better, he seems to have been an equal opportunity critic."

"He was plain mean," Franz said.

Elizabeth sat at one of the other chairs at the small table. "What can you tell me about yesterday?"

Franz shook her head. "No different than any other day. The mayor usually came in, of course."

"But not every day?" Elizabeth asked.

"She's an elected official, and most of the administrative responsibilities are with the city clerk. Another mayor, before you were here, Mayor Carmichael, tried to get the council to change it to a city manager position. That's more common today."

"Why didn't they?"

"Dingle and a few of his buddies fought it. Between you and me, I don't think he would have qualified to be a city manager. I guess Mayor Carmichael decided to wait until Dingle retired."

"But Carmichael left first," Elizabeth said.

"He and his wife decided to divorce. Friendly, from what I heard. Dingle started telling people his wife had an affair. Carmichael shoved him against the wall in Dingle's office."

Elizabeth let out a low whistle. "I never heard that."

"It was hushed up. Dingle acted like he was deeply offended, and he was doing Carmichael a favor not to bring in the police. Carmichael didn't run again, and Mayor Humphrey got elected."

Elizabeth leaned back in her chair. "You were here when I came to town."

She nodded. "I've been here six years. I'd have left, but my son loves his school, and he doesn't make friends easily. And my mother moved here when I did. I'd be messing up her life, too."

"Did you ever hear anyone threaten Donald Dingle?"

She laughed. "You mean to his face?"

Elizabeth smiled. "Or behind his back – meaningfully."

She shook her head slowly. "He probably fought most with Mayor Humphrey and me, but that's just because we sit in the executive suite with him. I've said things like I wished he'd break a hip and be forced to retire."

Elizabeth nodded. "Besides that kind of thing."

"No, everyone just tried to stay away from him."

CHAPTER NINE

AFTER ANOTHER FIFTEEN MINUTES going through Dingle's very neat desk, and deciding he was a closet choc-o-holic, Elizabeth shut his office door and turned the lock on the handle.

"Ms. Maitlin, could you call one of my guys and ask them to come over to put some crime scene tape across the door? They don't have to do it immediately."

"It's Carol, and of course."

"Thanks." Elizabeth turned toward the mayor's closed door. She needed to put aside her anger about Mayor Humphrey's actions yesterday. Usually she found that easier to do. She knocked on the mayor's door. "May I come in?"

"Please do."

Elizabeth opened the door and Humphrey gestured to a chair across from her desk. "Have a seat."

Elizabeth often briefed the mayor in her office. It looked little different from other staff offices and was not much larger than Dingle's. Other than the more expensive carpet and framed photos of various ground-breaking events, the office could have belonged to any city official.

Final Operation

"Before we talk about Donald Dingle, have you any idea who wrote that awful letter to the editor?" Humphrey asked.

Elizabeth shrugged. She wasn't about to say she thought Jerry Pew did it. "No. I expect it'll generate a few responses. Jerry'll like that."

Humphrey tapped a forefinger on her desk. "I gave him an earful. He should correct false information in those letters. Those eight officers work on three shifts!"

"I've heard his position on correcting letter-writers. He says it's their opinion and he only edits for length and hate talk. Thanks for the defense, but it'll blow over."

Humphrey closed her eyes and rubbed one temple with the same forefinger. "Have you learned much?"

Elizabeth had already decided everyone who'd been in contact with Dingle yesterday had to be a suspect. "Not too much. Mahan and Calderone are at the hospital doing interviews. I'd like you to think of anyone you saw near Mr. Dingle yesterday – from just before your argument with him…"

Mayor Humphrey winced.

"…to the time you walked in his room and found him."

Humphrey pulled a folded piece of paper from under her desk blotter. "I think they're all people you'd expect." She handed the list across her desk. "And I noted when I was with him."

Elizabeth studied it, saying nothing at first. "So you actually talked to him before they put the stents in?"

"Just for a minute, in his little room in the ER. He doesn't have any family. Much as I disliked him, I thought someone he knew should be with him. But a man came in almost right away to get him."

"How did Mr. Dingle seem to you?"

"Very tired, and very pale. I told him I wouldn't let anyone in his office while he was away. He locked the door every night."

"Is that common in City Hall?"

She shook her head. "In a suite like this, where the main door is locked after hours, it's not common. Only in places involving money. File cabinets or desks are locked, but not doors. Ms. Franz and I leave our doors unlocked."

Elizabeth smiled. "Nothing to hide?"

"That, and nothing anyone would want to take. One of the file cabinets in my office is actually more like a safe. Very heavy, the lock requires a combination, not just a key."

Elizabeth nodded. "I've noticed that. The dial is embedded in the cabinet. Any security issues?"

"Not that I know of."

"May I ask what you were fighting about?"

The mayor waved one hand, as if dismissing the question. "Mostly about him developing this whole...thing about getting rid of the police without consulting me. No one elected him to anything. It wasn't his place."

Elizabeth went back to the mayor's list. "You mentioned that after he had surgery, you saw the cardiologist go into Dingle's room before you did, and a nurse. No one else?"

"When he flat lined all hell broke loose. Before that, no one paid much attention to him after they got him settled."

"How long were you with him before you called to the nurse?"

She glanced at the clock on the wall and back to Elizabeth. "Maybe a minute, maybe less."

Elizabeth nodded. "A nurse mentioned she saw you send a text? Or at least typing into your phone."

For a moment the mayor's expression seemed blank. Then she raised her eyebrows. "Oh. I forgot. I texted Carol Maitlin to say I was with him. How could I have forgotten that?"

Elizabeth wondered the same thing, but said, "You probably would have remembered in an hour and called me."

The mayor leaned back in her chair and closed her eyes for a second. "Very stressful day."

"It is. One more thing. How easy was it to get in his room?"

Humphrey shrugged. "Like any hospital room. Anyone walking by could go in."

ELIZABETH ASKED HARMONY WILSON and Carol Maitlin if anyone they didn't know had been in the suite not long before Dingle collapsed.

Final Operation

Carol Maitlin, whom Elizabeth had always thought of as very precise, tilted her head to one side. "If anything, it was more quiet than usual." She smoothed the hem on her linen skirt.

"The mail hadn't even come yet," Wilson said.

Elizabeth glanced at the mayor's door, which she had closed. "Did you hear any of their argument?"

Wilson's shoulders hunched slightly. She reached into the middle drawer of her desk and pulled out two small, cylinder-shaped pieces of foam. "When they really get yelling I put in these earplugs."

When Elizabeth smiled, she added, "I can still hear if people walk up to my desk. I just can't stand the fighting. It reminds me of..." she stopped.

"You don't need to say what," Elizabeth said. She turned to Maitlin. "And did you hear much?"

She nodded. "Not every word." She glanced toward her feet. "I turn on a little fan under my desk. Mostly it was about the police stuff and Dingle not releasing the money for the nurse at the health center. The mayor said once she and the council made a decision, he was to make it happen."

Wilson nodded. "Implement it. She told him that a lot."

"Anything else?"

Maitlin looked toward the mayor's closed door. "From what the mayor said, I think he saw something in her desk, and she didn't like that."

"Is her desk locked?" Elizabeth asked.

"Not during the day and generally we'd feel free to open a drawer if we thought we knew where something was that we needed, or to put something in a drawer if she didn't want it to be put on her desk."

"Was that common?"

Maitlin and Wilson exchanged glances, and Wilson said, "Especially when Mr. Dingle wasn't in his office, this is a pretty friendly place. No one snoops, of course, but I don't think any of us hide anything from each other."

"Okay," Elizabeth said, "so they fought, and maybe Dingle had seen something she didn't want him to see?"

Maitlin shrugged. "Or maybe he just wanted to creep her out by saying he'd been in her desk. It's the first time I've heard her say he should be fired. And she said she could do it."

Elizabeth considered that. Dingle was a city employee, so it wasn't that simple. However, the mayor could probably remove him temporarily, and he could appeal an impending dismissal even as she might work with the city attorney to dot her i's.

"Did she say why she especially wanted to fire him now?" she asked.

Maitlin cocked her head, thinking. "I didn't hear all of it, but I think most of it was about the nurse position he withheld funds from."

Before Elizabeth could ask anything else, Maitlin said, "Please don't tell the mayor I heard them talk about her desk. She does lock it sometimes."

"Sure. I forgot to ask the mayor if she came back to work after Mr. Dingle went to the hospital."

Both women nodded. "She wanted to tell us how he was," Wilson said.

"She stayed for about half-an-hour. She left but came back."

"Right," Wilson said. "She said she realized she was more upset than she thought about him collapsing in front of her. I made her a cup of coffee. Then she went back. She wanted to be there when they were done with his surgery."

Elizabeth pulled two business cards from her blazer's pocket. "Okay. I don't want either of you playing investigator, but if you hear anything relevant, let me know."

"I certainly will," Maitlin said.

"How do you mean 'relevant'?" asked Wilson.

"If someone is behaving differently than you would expect in terms of Mr. Dingle or his death."

"No one cried," Wilson said.

"I'm not sure I would expect anyone to cry," Maitlin said.

WHEN ELIZABETH RETURNED TO the station at noon, a man sat in the public area. In Logland, only funeral home staff wore three-piece suits. Most business men and women wore what in a city would be called business casual, unless they were about to make a big sale or attend a formal meeting.

The fortyish man stood and extended a hand. "Chief Friedman, I presume."

Elizabeth felt like asking if he'd heard there was more than one female police officer in town. Instead, she shook his hand. "And you are?"

"Adam Kramer from the Hospital's Board of Directors. I chair the Oversight Committee. May I ask you a few questions?"

Elizabeth gestured to the gate that separated the public and private segments of the station. "I don't have a lot of time, but a few questions would be all right."

As they entered the bullpen she glanced at Hammer. He sat behind his desk, arms folded, and shrugged almost imperceptibly. "Mr. Kramer asked that I not notify you he was here."

Elizabeth rolled her eyes in Hammer's direction, which Kramer couldn't see. She preceded him into her office. "What's with the cloak and dagger?"

Kramer took a chair across from Elizabeth. He stiffened. "I always find privacy is best in our work."

Elizabeth sat behind her desk. "What's your topic?"

"Why, murder, of course. I believe this is the first such crime committed in Logland Memorial Hospital."

She nodded. "Ask away."

"First, I wanted to let you know that when the Oversight Committee looks into circumstances surrounding the death of Donald Dingle, we have no intention of intervening in police business."

Elizabeth let that sink in. She had anticipated an internal hospital review of some sort. "Thank you. I'm sure you'll delve more into the medical aspects of his death than we will, but there may be points at which we can help each other."

"Possibly. The key point for us is not just how the foreign substance was delivered to the patient, but how there could have been the opportunity for that action to be undertaken."

Elizabeth thought that Kramer must write a lot of academic papers. "I'm sure you've talked to Randall Watson in the hospital security office.

Kramer nodded. "And he informed me that your officer had already reviewed security footage of Mr. Dingle's time in the hospital."

"What footage there is. Do you know of more?"

"No. Much of our work will be comprised of in-depth interviews with staff"

Elizabeth leaned back in her chair and laced her fingers behind her head. "We've already done some of that, but we're largely focused on people who were in close proximity to Donald Dingle in the hours before he died. When we get more information from Dr. Curran, it could narrow the timeframe. I'm sure you'll have access to her report."

"Yes. Do you expect to identify the individual who injected him with the foreign substance?"

"Vodka, Mr. Kramer, vodka. And that's our goal. I rarely make promises because I can't control most of the circumstances of an investigation. We do our best."

Kramer cleared his throat. "My primary purpose in meeting is to inquire as to whether you would share information from your investigation."

"Yes and no. Perhaps some basic facts, if we don't think it will impinge on our work. Not conclusions until about the time we're ready to make them public."

He scowled. "Of course, you need hospital permission to be on the property."

Elizabeth thought she heard Hargrove's influence in his tone. "Police are rarely denied access to crime scenes unless, for example, we would risk toxic chemical exposure." She smiled briefly. "We respect that a hospital has many operational considerations. I have no problem setting up appointments, at my convenience, for staff to come here."

Kramer reddened. "I'm not talking about denying access…"

"No," Elizabeth said, "you're talking about controlling it. We will go where we need to, when we need to, to find Mr. Dingle's murderer. If necessary, we'll get warrants."

"Well, well…"

"Mr. Kramer, what are you trying to hide?"

He half-stood, than sat again. "Hide! We will cooperate fully."

Elizabeth stood. "Good." She walked to the side of her desk and extended a hand. We will let Mr. Hargrove know when we'll be in the building."

He shook her hand. "The sooner this business is resolved the sooner we can reassure patients."

Elizabeth smiled. "You aren't telling me the hospital is shuttered until the killer is found."

Kramer's smile was thin and brief. "So far, the only people who will be on administrative leave are Doctors Prasad and Hutton, and the Recovery Room nurse, Norma Norton."

Kramer left, and Elizabeth spent several minutes weighing the impact of the three suspensions – or whatever they were. She expected Dr. Prasad's loss would quickly be felt. She knew little of hospital dealings, but newspaper display ads featured his smiling face to encourage people to see a local cardiologist rather than travel to Springfield or St. Louis.

A heart attack patient would still be brought to the closest hospital. But if the hospital was down one cardiologist and it took a long time to schedule routine procedures, people would travel. She shook her head. *Not my problem.*

She turned on her computer and began to type an email to the head of the state crime lab. She thought that the best chance for fingerprints on syringes would be a thumb print where a nurse pressed when injecting the medicine. They usually had one hand on the patient's arm, or wherever, and the sides of two fingers steadying the base of the syringe.

Elizabeth had shaken the box. She guessed it held fifteen to twenty used syringes. Medical waste. She didn't think her staff had the expertise to handle the items, and wondered if there could be dangers beyond a needle stick. Would there be a risk of disease transmission? Heck, had the state lab ever gotten useful latent prints from a syringe?

She finished the email and was about to pick up the phone when she heard Hammer's raised voice. She thought the other belonged to Adrian Gangle. She stood and walked to the bullpen.

Gangle stood on the public side of the counter, red-faced and angry. He spotted Elizabeth. "What the hell does he mean, I have to schedule an appointment?"

Elizabeth approached him, careful not to smile. "It means that especially when we have an ongoing murder investigation I'm in and out of the office, and sometimes can't immediately see people." She said nothing else.

Gangle stiffened and pursed his lips. "You're here now."

Elizabeth nodded and gestured to the swinging half door at the end of the counter. "Come on back."

Gangle squared his shoulders and almost marched behind the counter. Elizabeth gestured that he should follow her and led the way to her office.

When they were both seated, she asked, "Is there something you want to talk about?"

"I want to know when you'll arrest Donald Dingle's killer!"

Elizabeth studied him for several seconds. He always wore a collared shirt, rarely with even a loosely knotted tie. He seemed to have gained weight, as the buttons across his chest fastened, but the two sides of his shirt over his stomach didn't quite meet.

"We are pursuing many lines of inquiry."

Gangle leaned toward her. "The sheriff would do better."

She held his gaze. "To date we've interviewed nineteen people and have a dozen more scheduled for later today. I doubt the sheriff would have the resources to undertake the intense interview schedule we'll handle the first few days."

Gangle stood. "I'll expect your briefing."

Elizabeth stood as well. "I brief the mayor. She sometimes chooses to have others present."

"We'll see about that!" He walked with balled fists as he left the station.

Elizabeth stared at her cabinet for several seconds. Did Gangle care about the man he often sided with for budget cuts or to question a department head's performance? She doubted it.

Her phone's intercom buzzed. "Yes, Hammer?"

"Our favorite campus cop is on the phone for you."

Elizabeth smiled. "Put Wally through."

"Afternoon, Chief. Sorry you have another murder to solve."

"Me, too, Officer Kermit." Elizabeth – all of her officers – had laughed at Wally's sometimes well-intentioned-but-off-base methods of law enforcement. He was definitely more adept at his other college position, that of part-time chemistry instructor.

"Now Chief, you know it's Wally."

"Sure. What's up?"

He hesitated. "Well now, this is a tough one."

"You guys still keeping your eyes open for the president's briefcase?"

"I found it this morning, in the ag barn, under a bunch of hay we spread for the pigs to lie in."

"That's great," Elizabeth said.

"I'm not sure you'll think so when you see what's in it."

CHAPTER TEN

WHEN CALDERONE AND MAHAN returned to Elizabeth's office at two Wednesday afternoon, they had little added information – beyond the hospital buzzing about the three staff being put on paid leave.

"I'm going to turn the intercom on, so Hammer can hear us. If it gets busy out there, I'll turn it off."

"I gave him a copy of this." Calderone passed her a copy of the Dingle Timeline, as he and Mahan dubbed their assessment of the city clerk's movements from collapse at City Hall to his death.

Elizabeth turned on the intercom and told Hammer to leave the channel open. Then she began to read.

- Ambulance called to City Hall, mayor's office. (8:15 AM)
- Ambulance arrived, IV inserted, Dingle stabilized.
- Ambulance left City Hall (8:35 AM)
- Dingle gets to the ER, hooked up to monitors (8:50 AM)
- Initial 'work up' by ER staff. Tightness and short of breath. Not much pain.

- Nitroglycerin given. Helped some. (9:10 AM)
- Bloodwork taken (same time as nitro)
- Portable x-ray brought to ER
- Cardiology doc (Prasad) visit to ER (9:55 AM)
- Decision made to wait for bloodwork, but probably check his arteries in the Cath Lab, maybe do stents

"What the heck is the Cardiac Cath Lab, anyway?" Mahan asked.

"I can answer that." Calderone said. "Cath is short for catheterization. They use a tiny instrument to thread its way toward your heart. It looks for blockages, opens 'em up with a stent."

Mahan screwed up his face. "Doesn't sound any better than the other kind of catheter-thing I've heard about."

"Same principle," Elizabeth said, dryly. "Different entry point."

Calderone laughed. "At least they go in through an artery."

"I've heard enough," Mahan said.

Elizabeth met Calderone's gaze.

He grinned. "I had a stent put in about eight years ago. This is a less stressful place to work since you got here."

"How come I didn't know that?" Mahan asked.

Calderone smiled. "Because it was none of your beeswax?"

Mahan frowned at him.

Calderone shrugged. "If anyone knew, it might've gotten back to our friendly former chief. He would've used it against me."

When Elizabeth arrived, she had thought the eight officers lacked ambition, even initiative. It didn't take long to learn that her predecessor had been overbearing and quick to criticize. The best stance, from his employees' points of view, was not to do anything that would get his attention.

No one lacked initiative now. Maybe the primary night patrol officer, Grayson, but when he was fully alert he was as good as the others.

"Let's get back to the timeline, gentlemen."

- Dingle stays in ER, awake some, dozing. Staff check him with monitors, some in person. About two hours. (Until about Noon)

"Why didn't they take him to get his arteries checked out right away?" Elizabeth asked.

"He ate breakfast," Mahan said. "They wanted to let it digest. Plus doctor schedule stuff, I think."

"Some blood enzymes can show a heart attack," Calderone said. "That's why they wanted to see those results."

"You should know," Mahan muttered.

Elizabeth nodded and started to go back to the timeline. She looked up. "Could they see who went in and out of his cubicle between the time the cardiologist left and Dingle was taken to his procedure?"

"Sometimes," Calderone said. "You can see it from one corner of the big staff work space, but there wasn't always someone in that corner."

"And not everybody came in the main ER door," Mahan added.

Elizabeth had been in the ER treatment space a number of times. She sat still for a moment, envisioning the layout. "I remember there's one door that leads to the corridor that goes down to the operating rooms. Staff only area, I think."

"Yeah," Calderone said, "but after you pass the operating stuff, the corridor ends at the back of a hallway near the X-ray Department. You can enter there if you have one of those badge things. So, if you had on scrubs you could act like you belonged there and maybe follow someone in."

"Unlikely, but not impossible," Elizabeth said. "Maybe one of you can sit near there in civvies and see how often someone seems to enter without using their own badge."

Final Operation

Mahan raised a hand. "As long as it's a comfortable chair."

"Sheesh." Elizabeth studied the timeline again.

- Dingle complains about being thirsty, so staff tell him he must be feeling better. He wants to go home. (11 AM)
- Nurse gives Dingle a "very mild" sedative. (11:15 AM)
- Mayor allowed to visit him. Nurse escorts her, but leaves her with him. (Just before Noon)
- "Two minutes" later Cath Lab guy comes to take him away. Mayor leaves. (Noon)
- 2.5 hours for procedure and Recovery Room. [Didn't talk to them yet.]

"Didn't they let you talk to the Cath Lab people?" Elizabeth asked.

Mahan shook his head. "Procedures underway. Staff were busy."

"Get that scheduled," she said.

"Will do," Calderone said.

- Nurse Norton calls transport to take Dingle to his room on 3rd floor. (2:15 PM)
- Jordan Hicks arrives. Dingle barely awake. Mumbles. (2:30 PM)
- Elevator to 3rd floor. Wheel by nurses' station, nurse joins transport guy. (Soon after 2:30)
- "Slide" him into bed. Transport guy leaves. (2:40 PM)
- Nurse "makes sure everything is hooked up." He mumbles when she talks to him.
- Nurse leaves to get warm blanket, gone less than two minutes.
- Nurse puts on blanket, makes sure IV is "flowing" and returns to nurses' station. (About 2:50 PM)

- "About ten minutes later," mayor stops at nurses' station to see if she can visit him. They say yes, but not for long. (3 PM)
- Mayor with him "about five minutes" and she hollers for a nurse. (About 3 PM)
- Nurse checks, calls for assistance.
- They "don't do much" because he has a 'do not resuscitate' order. (Time of death called, 3:20 PM)

"Did anyone see him in those ten minutes before the mayor went in?" Elizabeth asked.

"Prasad went in for less than a minute." Mahan said. "No one remembers seeing anyone else go in there, but they said someone could have."

"Did you talk to any staff about your list?" Elizabeth asked.

"It's pretty much directly what they said. I think because he died the staff were willing to talk to us more than when we're in there after a bar brawl or something."

Elizabeth regarded the list again. "Lots of options for someone to get to him, but unfortunately for the mayor, she's the most obvious.

Hammer stood in the doorway to Elizabeth's office. "I didn't hear about any other city council members or employees stopping by the hospital, did you?"

Elizabeth had almost forgotten they were speaking so Hammer could hear them. "I don't think I did."

"The council people all have jobs, of course," Hammer said. "Even if they heard about it, they might have planned to go when they got off work."

"And since the mayor was at the hospital until he went for his operation, staff wouldn't have come down," Calderone said.

"Or wanted to," Mahan added."

When Mahan and Calderone left, Elizabeth spent ten minutes signing timecards and returning phone calls.

Hammer stuck his head into her office. "Philip Hargrove is on the line. I told him I wasn't sure you could talk just now."

"Not much to tell. Put him through."

Hargrove's official tone was in full use. "Chief. What do you have for me?"

Elizabeth wanted to remind him she didn't work for him. "Your staff have been helpful, but it doesn't bring us much closer to a killer."

"I'm sorry to hear that."

"Could be good news. I think everyone would like to believe that a health care worker would never kill a patient."

"Anything I should know?" Hargrove asked.

"Not yet. I may stop by myself to do a couple interviews."

"Fine. I'd like you to do something for me. It would be helpful if you could say you see no indication of hospital staff involvement. Could take some suspicion from the hospital and help us avoid regulatory interference."

Elizabeth did a brief internal debate on her next comment, but said it anyway. "Sir, we've never implicated hospital employees. I think when you suspended Nurse Norton and Doctors Prasad and Hutton, people assumed you thought the problem was at the hospital. If you were to issue a statement welcoming them back, it would do more than me saying we've eliminated any staff we've talked to."

The silence was so complete Elizabeth thought Hargrove had hung up.

He finally spoke. "When police are involved in a shooting, they go on leave."

"True. But they've definitely been involved in something awful, whether their role in it was correct or not. The doctors worked on or were near Mr. Dingle, but no one has indicated – to us – that they did something wrong."

"I would welcome your *information* as soon as you get it." Hargrove hung up.

Elizabeth shook her head as she replaced the receiver. "My information, not my opinion."

Hammer buzzed her. "Did he know something?"

"No, I think he wanted a PR-type statement from me saying we'd turned up nothing at the hospital. I suggested he shot himself in the foot with putting Skelly and Dr. Prasad on leave. He hung up."

Hammer laughed. "What a jerk."

AT FIVE O'CLOCK, ELIZABETH went through Wednesday's interviews. Each had a one-paragraph summary, saying how and when they interacted with Dingle. Most important, except when he was being transported from the Cath Lab to a private room, at least two hospital staff were with him.

Calderone and Mahan interviewed each hospital staffer together, and Mahan had written the interview notes for the transporters. Jordan Hicks had asked if Mahan knew his aunt, Margaret Turner. Mahan said no, but Elizabeth knew the woman.

Margaret Turner had told the City Council that her husband, Jordan's uncle, had a foot amputated. She believed the delay in getting an appointment at the health center contributed to needing the amputation. She blamed part of that delay on lower staffing levels, which she saw as partly the city's fault. More important, she thought that lost foot would keep her husband from playing basketball with Jordan.

Elizabeth pulled up the full interview notes from the office network. The hospital transporter had been quiet during the interview, volunteering nothing beyond what he'd been asked, and asking no questions. Most people asked the police if they were close to solving the crime.

She buzzed Calderone. "I just read some of Mahan's notes. How did Jordan Hicks strike you?"

He shrugged. "He didn't seem to care much about Dingle's death, but a lot of people wouldn't."

"Anything in his background to indicate he had a temper?"

"Nothing, but I can dig deeper," Calderone said.

"I think I'll talk to him, ask him whether he thinks underfunding at the health center contributed to his uncle's foot amputation."

"You think he'll let on if he's mad about it?"

Elizabeth sat back in her chair and stared at the screen. "Maybe, maybe not. I'll watch for body language when I ask questions."

"You really think he could have killed Dingle?" Calderone asked.

"I think he would have had the opportunity, but you have to hope the average hospital employee isn't walking around with vodka in their pocket."

CHAPTER ELEVEN

AT FIVE-FORTY-FIVE, Elizabeth closed her computer and headed for the Weed n' Feed. She thought Wally's choice of meeting place an odd one, but he had insisted, saying that university faculty didn't "frequent the place." Too many students.

Elizabeth got to the Weed n' Feed before Wally, so she stood near the breezy door and wondered how high the electric bill was. The scuffed wood floors and long bar were part of the place's appeal, but since pot had been legalized, the restaurant element had become equally popular. Nearly every table was full.

The door opened again. In blue jeans and a dark green polo shirt, thirty-ish Wally didn't look a lot older than some of the Sweathog College students.

Weed n' Feed Owner Harvey Hunter called to Elizabeth as she and Wally walked toward a booth. "Your regular, Chief?"

Smart bar owner who knows which beer the chief of police drinks. "Yes, thanks." Elizabeth was never sure if he called attention to her to warn patrons to tow some imaginary line, or let others know the local police chief thought the Weed n' Feed was totally above board.

"Thanks for meeting me here, Chief."

"It's Elizabeth, Wally. We aren't on duty."

"Right." He began to take papers from a manila folder, but stopped as Hunter placed a beer in front of Elizabeth.

"More where that came from, Chief. You guys want some food?"

"I've eaten," Wally said, "but I'll take a lite beer."

"How about some of your hot spinach dip and chips?" Elizabeth asked.

"You got it."

"Thanks, Harvey." She raised an eyebrow at Wally. "You still have some of Dodd's materials?"

"He doesn't know I've found the case. I'll give it all back tomorrow."

"It was unlocked?" Elizabeth asked.

"Still locked. Someone jimmied the hinges." He opened the folder and turned it to face her.

Elizabeth picked up the paper on top. The memo from Donald Dingle to President Dodd was one of his classic, backstabbing missives.

"Mr. President, thanks for your enthusiasm about absorbing some of the law enforcement duties now performed by the Logland Police Department. As we discussed, the Council could vote to broaden Campus Security's jurisdiction for five blocks extending from college boundaries. That coverage area would include much of the minor crime committed in Logland."

Elizabeth glanced at Wally. "You didn't know about this?"

"No. Can't imagine any other security staff did, either. There's only the four of us, all part-time."

Elizabeth murmured, "Even if the council wanted to do this, somebody'll file a lawsuit saying the city essentially reduced protection for citizens."

"As you indicated, we would need to discuss the rate of overhead. Even if it were to be a standard forty percent, I envision that the city-provided funds would be far less than money spent in the same coverage area under the current police department.

Elizabeth murmured, "I never knew Dingle was this dumb."

Wally shifted in his seat.

She raised her gaze to his. "The college would have to dedicate people to this one area. We spread out all over town. The city would spend a lot more by reimbursing the college just to cover one area of town."

Wally smiled. "Any teacher can do that math."

Elizabeth skimmed the rest of the two-page memo. Dodd had badly mischaracterized his discussion with Dingle about campus security. That had to be deliberate.

When she looked up, Wally said, "The thing is, the only reason people are willing to do security work sometimes is that you folks can get to campus within a few minutes. We've been to a couple of training courses, but we aren't police."

"Did you see anything in writing from Dodd to Dingle?"

Wally shook his head. "Dodd's too smart for…damn it to hell!" He stood up and looked under the booth's table. "Something furry's down there."

Elizabeth leaned over and saw two green eyes. "I think it's a cat."

"An effing cat?"

Harvey hurried over. "I've been looking for him."

Elizabeth tried not to smile too broadly. She had once found Wally on a table in the now-closed fraternity house because some goats wanted to be friendly. She looked down at Harvey who was reaching under the table. "Health Department allow cats in here?"

"God no. We feed him behind the building but he tries to sneak in."

"Succeeded," Elizabeth said.

Harvey had to slide the cat from under the table, its claws clicking on the floor. "Sorry." He stood, awkwardly. "Don't tell on us?"

"I won't," she said.

Harvey put the disgruntled feline over his shoulder. "Beer and chips are on the house."

"Not mine," Elizabeth said.

"Or mine." Wally sat down again. "Thought it was a big rat."

Still smiling, Elizabeth asked, "How does a guy at an agricultural college dislike animals so much."

Wally reddened. "No cows or pigs in a chemistry lab. I deal with fertilizer formulas and composition of different kinds of feed."

Elizabeth nodded. "I don't think Dingle's outsourcing ideas are going anywhere with the City Council, but...hey. What else was in the briefcase?"

"Mostly paperwork I didn't read because the folders said stuff like "employee ratings." Did you know Dodd was diabetic?"

Elizabeth smiled. "So, the syringes were in the briefcase?"

Wally frowned. "Syringes? No, just one vial of insulin."

"Damn. I'd be less concerned if the thief took the meds in addition to the needles."

Wally nodded slowly. "You think that's why the briefcase was stolen, to get the syringes?"

Elizabeth sipped her beer. "That would mean the perp knew the contents. Seems a lot of trouble to go to for a couple syringes."

"I figure someone saw the briefcase and took it." Wally half-shrugged. "Crime of opportunity."

"But why leave it in the hay?" Elizabeth asked.

"Makes me think it was a student who lived on campus. Didn't have his or her own car to hide it in, wasn't about to keep it in the dorm."

"Good thinking." She phrased her next question carefully. "We've talked before about you finding empty dime bags on campus, but there isn't a lot of IV drug use, is there?"

"I don't like the idea of people snorting coke on campus, but heroin's worse, and I think people are using it more."

"Why do you say that?"

"You know better than me that opioids are getting harder to get. I woke up a couple students in that tiny park area outside the cafeteria the other day. Figured they were lovebirds who fell asleep. But they were way too groggy."

"But no needles?" Elizabeth asked.

"Girl kept her purse too close. I figured their stuff was in there, but I didn't have any reason to search it. And it's a college campus. We aren't looking too hard at what people have for individual use. That's changing because heroin's so dangerous, but you still can't walk up to someone and ask them to empty their purse or pockets."

Elizabeth nodded, slowly. "I get it. But you don't witness sales, do you?"

Wally shook his head firmly. "Never. I didn't ask the pair to show me ID, because I didn't want them to think I'd single them out. I knew I could get their names later. I told the others guys. We're paying attention to them, but I doubt they'll use it in a public place again."

"That just means they won't be found if they OD."

"Yeah, and you know how deserted that campus is on weekends, except around the barns. And that's just a few of the animal husbandry students."

The almost nonexistent weekend life at the college had surprised Elizabeth when she moved to Logland. Then she'd learned that a lot of smaller rural-area colleges, especially community colleges, were the same way. Many students commuted. Libraries had shorter hours than during the week and the cafeterias served only the few students who stayed in the dorms.

"You guys don't even work on the weekends, do you?"

"Couple hours in the evening is all, and we just drive around some and check to be sure doors are locked. Mostly to show some presence." He grinned. "Nobody's up and around in the morning on weekends."

Elizabeth pointed to the manila folder. "I'd like to dust the briefcase that was in for prints."

"I did. Wiped clean, inside and out."

Elizabeth raised her eyebrows.

Wally flushed. "I've been taking online courses, bought some print powder and a brush, and the tape you use."

Elizabeth hid her annoyance. She would have preferred to have her officers check the briefcase. "Odd they took so much care. Almost makes me think the person's prints were already in the system." She paused. "I know you checked the case, but let's stop by the station to see if we can get anything."

Elizabeth called Mahan. "I know you haven't been home long, but could Wally meet you at the station to check that briefcase for prints?"

"Sure. Where'd he find it?"

Elizabeth winked at Wally. "I'll let him tell you."

ELIZABETH WISHED SHE HADN'T made plans to meet Skelly in the Bully Pulpit at seven. Nothing she said would appease his fury, so she didn't bother trying. She focused on the food Nick placed in front of them.

"Two days in a row to be told to leave my own autopsy rooms!"

She tried for a sympathetic expression. "Hopefully we'll get more concrete evidence about the real killer, and this will blow over."

Skelly waved a hand. "It makes no sense. They can contract out the occasional autopsy, but ER doctors are hard to come by. And a cardiologist? Keeping Dr. Prasad from working will cost the hospital a lot of patients. We're close enough to St. Louis and Springfield for people to go to heart docs there."

Elizabeth stabbed a cherry tomato. "I can't explain their decisions. They seem self-defeating."

Nick came to their booth, carrying a glass coffee pot with an orange handle. He knew Skelly usually wanted decaf in the evening, and she drank tea later in the day. "So, you arrested anybody, Chief?"

"Nope. What do you hear?"

Nick stopped mid-pour. "You mean, like, who did it?"

She smiled. "That would be the most helpful point, but all news is useful."

Skelly tapped his mug, and Nick continued pouring. "Everybody wants to know if a needle in the red box you took from the hospital was used to kill Mr. Dingle."

Elizabeth frowned. "Where'd you hear about a box of needles?"

Nick shrugged. "Everybody's talking about it. I don't remember who said, in particular."

"You know how police keep some information to themselves?" she asked.

"Yeah, kinda."

"This is one of those things. But if you hear anything, you can pass it to me. Or one of the others."

"Oh, I get it." He nodded at someone on the far side of the diner and walked toward them.

"Need your kitchen painted or anything?" Skelly asked.

"Aren't you on leave with pay?"

"Yeah, but I need to keep busy."

Elizabeth glanced over her shoulder and took in Nick, already deep in conversation with a man in a St. Louis Cardinals baseball cap. She looked back to Skelly. "A couple people have made comments about the nurse's appearance."

"Norton's? Like what?"

She shook her head. "I'm not going to suggest anything."

Skelly stared out the window for half a minute. "Okay, her pupils were smaller, but I don't really know her. Could be her normal."

"Or maybe she needed to get rid of a used syringe."

"But the sharps box was right there. If she had it in her purse she could have added it to the box."

"Unless when she heard Dingle died she was afraid she or her bag would be searched. Then she'd want a way to say a needle belonged to someone else."

"Can't prove it."

Elizabeth nodded. "I don't think I have to. If I let her know we don't suspect her of killing Dingle, she'll be more likely to tell the truth."

"If her accusation was deliberately false, she might get her ass fired. That's no incentive to change her story."

"Who's going to tell the hospital? If it's unrelated to Dingle's death, nothing has to appear in our police reports about a conversation about where a needle really came from."

Skelly laughed. "So you want me to get chummy with my accuser?"

"Happens in novels all the time."

"Only problem is, if she works at the hospital and has a drug problem, she gets one chance to kick it, with hospital support. Any relapse and she's canned."

"So you be the support."

"The things I do for you," Skelly said.

They ate in silence for a minute, Elizabeth again wondering how Skelly stayed in shape when he ate cheeseburgers four or five times a week. "What could she inject herself with that wouldn't make her drowsy at work?"

"You can inject cocaine, but it's a lot more dangerous than snorting or smoking it," Skelly said.

"So why do it?"

Skelly drained his decaf. "My guess would be that someone who works in a hospital would think it easier to spot the result of snorting it. You know, nosebleeds especially. Have a bleed at work and you're with people who want to look up your nose. They'd be able to tell."

"But there'd be track marks on her arms," Elizabeth said.

"Probably, but I can't think of a single nurse who wears short sleeves. It's always cold in that hospital."

Elizabeth took the last bite of her chicken gumbo soup. "Since that syringe probably doesn't relate to Dingle's death, it doesn't matter. I'd still like to know if she really found one, or if she made up the story."

Skelly saluted. "I'll do what I can."

Nick breezed past with a tray loaded with ice cream sundaes. "You guys be here another minute?"

Skelly said, "About five."

Elizabeth narrowed her eyes at Skelly. "Going somewhere?" She regretted her word choice immediately.

"As if. I don't want him thinking we'll be here all night. I have some detecting to do."

Elizabeth rolled her eyes. She looked in her purse for her billfold and took it out.

Nick, empty tray in hand, returned. "So, uh, you two would be good if I ask some questions?"

"Sure," Skelly said, and Elizabeth nodded.

"Like three times this evening I've heard people talkin' about how they're worried about getting poisoned at the hospital."

Skelly didn't take his eyes off of Nick, who continued.

"I would still go there. I mean, it was Mr. Dingle, right? Who else would a doc kill?"

Elizabeth coughed into her napkin to hide her laughter.

Skelly nodded. "Although Donald Dingle died at LMH, we don't actually know that a hospital staff member caused his death."

Nick frowned. "Huh. That makes it tough."

"What do you mean?" Elizabeth asked.

"Well, um, lots of people hated his guts."

Skelly grinned briefly. "We try to take good care of everyone. Elizabeth?"

"We've interviewed a lot of people, Nick. I can't tell you we'll arrest someone in three days. We're trying to narrow the pool of people who were with him that day."

"Okay." He frowned and tapped the tray against his thigh. "Can I tell people you're close?"

"Do people talk about it a lot?" she asked.

"Some to me. More to Marti. You know, it's kinda her job to talk a lot. To customers, I mean."

"Marti around?" Elizabeth asked.

"Nope. My night to close. We hired a couple dishwashers. College guys. I mean they don't work at the same time, but it helps to have someone cleaning the kitchen when it's only one of us here."

Elizabeth took money from her billfold. "Tell Marti to call me anytime. I'll make sure Sergeant Hammer knows to put her through even if I'm busy."

"Wow. She'll like that." He ambled away.

Elizabeth turned to Skelly. "I think people are more scared than I thought."

ELIZABETH HAD BEEN HOME for less than five minutes when Mahan called. "Wally was right about that briefcase being cleaned, but I found a single thumbprint, near the hinge on the bottom of the briefcase."

"Did you find a match?"

"Yep. We picked up the guy before for trying to drain anhydrous ammonia from a farmer's tank."

"Meth maker? Who is it?"

"Floyd Yeltsin, age fifty-two and a perpetual loser around town."

"How come I don't know him?" Elizabeth asked.

"He hasn't been arrested for a few years. Did a year up in Joliet about the time you got here, been done with parole for some time."

"So keeping his nose clean or not getting caught?"

"This would say the latter," Mahan said.

"Odd," Elizabeth said. "Since it was in the ag barn I assumed it would be a student."

"I've seen him work at the concession stand for football games a couple times. Probably knows his way around campus."

"So, he's looking for money to fund a habit, he's familiar with campus, and he decides to get into some unlocked cars to pick up cash. And then he ends up with this briefcase, but he definitely doesn't want to hang onto it."

"Could be," Mahan said. "And he figures nobody'll look for a briefcase in a barn."

"But why not just take it with him?"

"Well, lemme check the DMV stuff."

Elizabeth heard him tapping keys, then Mahan came back on the phone. "No tags or driver's license in his name. He maybe can't hide it in a trunk and doesn't want to carry it around."

"Okay. Thanks for doing this tonight. Come in an hour late tomorrow, and check him out. If he seems to be employed, don't wreck his rep with an employer. My bet is he's not working."

Mahan grunted. "Probably selling stuff off the books."

Elizabeth hung up. If Floyd Yeltsin was responsible for the break-ins it made sense that he had taken the syringes. But she still thought it was dumb to hide the briefcase in the hay in the ag barn. She realized she was trying to make sense of what a likely druggie had done, and there could be little logic to his choice.

Lucky meowed and she looked down at her. "It would be nice to close out the car break-ins."

She meowed again and put a paw on Elizabeth's shoe.

"You had plenty. You want to trade jobs? I'll stay home all day and sleep in the window and you figure out who killed Dingle. Do it soon and I'll buy you a whole case of canned Friskies."

CHAPTER TWELVE

ELIZABETH GOT UP THURSDAY morning and turned on the 6 AM television news. She almost spit out her coffee when she saw the lead story.

"Sources in city government tell our news team that police in Logland have made no progress in catching the killer of Donald Dingle, the town's city clerk. We have learned that while he died in the hospital, his death is not believed to be connected to a cardiac procedure he underwent earlier in the day."

Sources in city government!

"With the lack of resolution comes growing concern among residents who wonder how safe they are at Logland Memorial Hospital. Rumors swirl in this small town south of Springfield as the hospital has begun an independent investigation of circumstances surrounding..."

Elizabeth clicked off the television. She had planned to talk to Jordan Hicks to decide for herself if he should be a suspect. Now maybe she should issue some sort of statement beyond something like "investigating all avenues."

Her cell phone rang. Skelly.

"Did you see the news?"

"Just now. What do you think the impact will be?"

"I know part of it. Hargrove called me when the 6 AM story was still on. Said he was going to wait until later in the day, but he decided to let me know I was no longer on leave. His words."

"That's terrific. How about Dr. Prasad?"

Skelly snorted. "I asked. He told me personnel matters were confi…I'm getting another…Ha! It's Prasad. I'll call you back."

Elizabeth finished getting dressed. Since she planned to go to the hospital, she wore a deep purple pants suit with a cream, long-sleeved top. She didn't want to scare the patients.

She had just picked up her car keys when Skelly called back. "You didn't tell me you told Hargrove he was an ass for putting us on leave."

"Those weren't my exact words. How did you find out?"

"He told Prasad you suggested that public perception might have been misinformed when he placed us on leave."

"I think I suggested he created the perception someone at the hospital was guilty."

"Either way, I have an ER shift today. I owe you. Think about how you want to collect."

Collect indeed, she thought. But she didn't need to come up with any ideas because Skelly called when she got to the station.

Irritation flowed from every word. "You know that so-called Oversight Committee that's looking into Dingle's death?"

"Sure, Kramer stopped by a few days ago to say they wouldn't interfere with what we're doing. Seemed kind of ingratiating."

"They aren't worried about my gratitude. Apparently they heard Prasad and I were back on board, and told the Board of Directors they thought I might be – and this is a quote – 'somehow involved in Patient Dingle's death, and it could be a risk to patients to have me treat them.' The Board President ordered Hargrove to put me back on leave."

"Any reason given for why they think you're involved?"

Skelly's voice rose. "No, and I'm not to talk to anyone on the board or their damn Oversight Committee."

"I can probably find out something, though not today. I don't want to appear to be acting on your behalf."

"Sheesh. I get it. I'm beginning to think no matter how this turns out I need to think about working elsewhere. These insinuations could follow me around Logland for years."

The thought of Skelly moving disheartened Elizabeth. To take her mind off him, she turned to the interview notes, which almost filled a two-inch binder. Elizabeth had done the ones with city officials, and Mahan and Calderone had cornered mostly hospital staff. She wrote an email to both asking for details on how a patient's medications were secured during and after an operation. Could a killer have put vodka in an empty vial labeled for something else?

She sent the email and stared at her computer monitor as she thought about Skelly having to leave Logland. She was friendly with a number of people, but he was her only real friend in town. A friend she felt conflicted about.

She pushed back from her computer and buzzed Hammer. When he stuck his head in her office, she asked, "You hear much about this Kramer guy who was in here, and the review a hospital Oversight Committee is doing?"

"Nope. You want me to ask around?"

Elizabeth shook her head. "Probably needs to be at my pay grade."

Hammer grinned. "Good. I didn't like the guy."

"Yeah, kind of a brown-noser. One more thing. Did Mahan tell you this Floyd Yeltsin likely took Dodd's briefcase?"

"Yeah. Said he was going to pay attention to him for a couple days. Whatever that means."

"I told him to try not to roust him at work. Don't want to maybe cost him a job if there's some innocuous reason his print should be on Dodd's briefcase."

"You really think that's possible?"

"No. And I can't see any link between the briefcase and the murder, but it's odd that the case had insulin syringes and Dingle was injected or whatever."

Hammer's look said her thinking was far-fetched. She changed the subject. "I read notes from interviews with public works staff. Nothing jumped out at me. Did you get something set up with the director?"

"Yeah, he said he's sorry he wasn't available yesterday. Something about March potholes and a stretch of sidewalk put in last fall that settled so much you almost have to walk sideways."

"Where is it?" Elizabeth asked.

"On the side of the square that has that sort of quilty sewing store."

Elizabeth smiled. "Lots of older people go in and out of that store. Did he ask us to do anything?"

Hammer laughed. "No. I'll alert the EMTs to be on call."

"I haven't seen notes on Dingle's house. Who went over there?"

"I think Taylor did. He doesn't type them up too fast."

"Just for fun, tell me why our school resource officer checked the victim's home?"

"I think Mahan and Calderone were going every which way. I'll tell him you need his notes."

"Okay. Make it clear I want them before he leaves today."

Taylor was a competent officer, and especially good with teenagers. But one reason he was the eyes and ears and relationship-builder at the schools was because he wasn't a great interviewer. His writing skills were also far from perfect. She sometimes heard about an issue at a school only when an assistant principal called to compliment Taylor on preventing a cafeteria fight, or something similar, but he hadn't written it up.

If Taylor had found an abandoned pet or anything amiss at Dingle's place, he would have told her. No matter what Taylor found, she'd check out the house herself.

WHILE SHE WAITED ON the straight-backed chair outsides Milton Weeks' office, Elizabeth had time to look around the dingy space. She hadn't realized that the head of Public Works operated out of such a small space in the maintenance garage. She'd never looked for him.

The metal desk in the small outer office where she sat held six clipboards with work orders, each labeled by type of work –

plumbing, carpentry, streets and snow removal, electrical, lawn/gardens, and Dingle's Office. In the corner sat a battery that looked as if it would fit a riding mower. She couldn't read the sticky note attached to it.

Weeks' voice drifted in. "I can't now, Simmons, I have a meeting with Chief Friedman." Weeks barreled into the small space and stopped a few feet from Elizabeth, as she stood. "Sorry to be late, Chief."

"It's Elizabeth, remember? And you aren't. I finished something else a few minutes early."

He gestured that she should precede him into his office, which was as crowded as the waiting room, but seemed more orderly. Half the room was taken up by gray, four-drawer file cabinets. "Can I get you coffee? We have a pot near the microwave in the garage."

"No thanks. I need to talk to you about Donald Dingle."

He sat behind a larger gray, metal desk and Elizabeth sat across from him in a chair that had a dark spot on it.

He saw her glance at it. "Old oil stain. Won't get on your clothes. I figure you heard him and me went at it sometimes."

"I heard he was pretty rude to you. You've put up with it for a long time."

"Yeah. Couple times I almost threw in the towel and applied to work as a custodian at the high school. But I was damned if Dingle was gonna run me out of my job. Besides," he pointed to a lower drawer in his desk, "I keep mother's little helper down there for the worst days. Not too often."

Elizabeth frowned slightly. "In the Rolling Stones song, that means pot."

"Oh, damn." He laughed. "I'm not so hip. I take a small nip now and again." He took a key out of his middle desk drawer and opened the bottom drawer and pointed.

Elizabeth leaned over and saw four, single-serving sized bottles of wine. *Oh, good. Telling the chief of police you keep alcohol in your desk.* "I can, uh, see how that might help."

He shut the drawer. "I only drink at lunch or after official work hours."

Somehow Elizabeth doubted that, but didn't feel like complicating her life by pointing out city rules on alcohol in the office. "Did you happen to see Dingle the day he died?"

Weeks shook his head. "Had two messages on my phone. He said the door to the mayor's office squeaked and it annoyed him, so I should oil it."

"Her office, not his?" Elizabeth asked.

"Yep. You know he minded everybody else's business. Other message was that a lightbulb needed changed in one of those pole lamps just outside the entrance to City Hall."

"He called you personally for stuff like that?"

"Oh, yeah. And he expected me to jump even if a pipe broke in a bathroom or something big like that."

Elizabeth shook her head. "I've heard people say how good you were about not responding to his temper. Did you ever hear anyone threaten him or, I have to ask, did you?"

He grinned and picked up a coffee cup, saw it was empty and replaced it on his desk. "Not out loud." He grew somber. "Lots of people said…I guess you'd say outrageous stuff. Not something they'd really do."

"Like what?"

"Well…like a couple weeks ago he said he wanted some trim, ceiling trim, nailed in better in the procurement office. When I told Lonnie to go do it, he asked if he could plant a nail in Dingle. Now he didn't really want to do that."

Elizabeth nodded and smiled. "I hear you. Any more realistic comments?"

"Nah. I tried to always be the buffer. 'Course, he was the butt of a lot of jokes, guess you'd say some pranks."

"Pranks?"

Weeks shrugged. "Couple years ago the guys asked me if they could plant some bulbs under his window. You know, tulips in spring, then they'd put in some annuals."

Elizabeth furrowed her brow. "He liked flowers?"

Weeks snorted. "I doubt he could name any. Let's just say the guys made sure they applied heavy amounts of mushroom soil under his window."

Elizabeth laughed. "Nice and smelly, huh?"

"Yep. They always put down a little more right before a heat wave."

"Inventive. Well, he wasn't killed with excrement."

"What did kill him?" Weeks asked. "Lots of rumors."

"Not certain yet, but it appears something unhealthy was put into his blood."

"Huh. At the hospital?"

"Probably," Elizabeth said, "but we can't be sure where, and certainly don't know who did it -- yet."

"Huh. Well, I was in a bunch of places that day, if you need an alibi for me."

"Not this minute. Shoot me an email of your schedule." She smiled. "You don't appear on any hospital security cameras."

"Jeez."

Elizabeth had planned to ask her next questions casually. "Your son works at the hospital, doesn't he?"

"Robert, yes. He's a senior paramedic now."

"Did you get a chance to talk to him when Dingle was in the ER?"

"Oh, sure. Called him as soon as I heard Dingle'd been taken over there. Kind of frustrating though. He takes the patient privacy stuff pretty seriously. Wouldn't tell me much."

Elizabeth wanted to ask if he'd suggested his son spike Dingle's blood. "Good that he's so professional. If someone treated my father the way Dingle treated you, I'd be tempted to get even."

Weeks shrugged. "Robert doesn't let a lot get to him."

She smiled. "Back to business. Can you think of anyone who might have been angry enough to want Dingle dead?"

Weeks leaned back in his chair, which squeaked. "I don't know anyone who liked the guy. He fought with anyone he thought he should be able to boss and couldn't. Like the mayor. But I can't see her doing something like that."

"Who did he argue with the most?"

"Well, I didn't argue back much, but the people he chewed out most were me and the budget woman, Franz. I mean, we reported to him, so he was pretty damn critical."

Elizabeth shook her head. "I'm sorry you had to put up with that."

Weeks shrugged. "I figured he'd retire long before me. You got any actual suspects?"

"Nothing solid." *More like nothing at all.*

CHAPTER THIRTEEN

ELIZABETH CALLED THE HOSPITAL Thursday morning to let Hargrove's secretary know she would be talking to transport staff.

"I'll tell him," the secretary said. "Do you want someone to go with you?"

"No thanks. I just have a couple background questions."

As Elizabeth drove to the hospital she heard a text message beep. She parked and read Calderone's note about how patient medications were secured.

The ones used in the operating room were sealed until use, and there would have been more than one person around when they were opened. Liquid meds for patients on the floors were handled similarly, with each patient's medications stored separately. Dingle didn't have time to receive any kind of medicine after he got to his room on the Cardiac Unit.

When she got to the hospital front desk, Elizabeth asked for directions to the manager who oversaw the transport staffers.

"They're officially under the chief nurse administrator, but they park in the back of the ER. They help move ER patients to x-ray and wherever when they aren't moving people on the floors."

"Ah. I'll head down there." She walked to the elevator.

Already in there was a tall, brown-haired woman in scrubs. She carried a plastic caddy with tubes to draw blood, alcohol pads, cotton balls, and other paraphernalia. While most of the caddy was open, one portion was fastened. Elizabeth supposed the needles were in that section.

"Chief Friedman, right?"

"Yes." She glanced at the woman's hospital badge. "I'm going to take a wild guess, Felicity, and say that you're on the way to draw blood."

"I'm heading to the ER. Do you mind if I ask if you've arrested anyone for the patient's murder?"

Elizabeth shook her head. "Not yet. We will."

"We hear all kinds of things."

Elizabeth tried to make her smile reassuring. "We will learn more, but I hear it's gotten to be common knowledge that someone injected him with something that ought not to have been swirling in his blood."

"We heard alcohol."

Elizabeth nodded. "It seems so. But we won't have full details until we get a report later this week. Please don't quote me."

"Someone did it when he was in here?"

"Can't be sure yet. When we know the concentration in the blood, we'll know more."

Felicity smiled. "Blood tells all."

They got off the elevator and Elizabeth stopped at the water fountain as Felicity used her badge to enter the ER treatment area.

How easy would it be to swipe a syringe from a phlebotomist? That would point to a hospital employee, though surely they would have other ways to get a syringe, with or without a needle.

Elizabeth headed to the ER receptionist and said she wanted to talk to patient transporters to get some background information.

Final Operation

The receptionist seemed to debate the point with herself. "You aren't here to arrest anybody or something, are you? Cause none of us think anyone here hurt that man."

Elizabeth shook her head. "No arrests. Just wanted some help. Jordan Hicks around?"

The receptionist picked up a self-adhesive badge that said "Visitor" and wrote "Chief Friedman" on it. "Since you aren't with a patient, it's important that you wear this in the ER. I can call back for you."

"I don't want to alarm him. I'll walk back."

"Take a right as you walk in, then another just past the nurse's station. At the back is a sort of hallway that usually has a few gurneys sitting there. He'll be in a chair near there." She grinned. "Or flirting with a red-headed nurse in brown scrubs."

"I'll try not to interrupt that."

The receptionist buzzed her through. Without her uniform, no one paid much attention to her, and Elizabeth followed the receptionist's directions. Jordan stood next to a chair, looking out a window at the now barren corn field behind the hospital.

When she got closer, Elizabeth said, "Jordan, I hope you can help me with some information."

He turned to face her, expression impassive. Hicks stood nearly six feet and his unruly black curls went in ten directions. He arched his eyebrows. "Chief Friedman. You need my help? You mean in your investigation?"

Elizabeth stood next to him and looked out the window. He turned again and did the same. "You know a lot of people, and you've been in the community health center with your aunt and uncle, I think."

"Not my favorite place. And your guy Dingle didn't help it any."

"I got that from your aunt's presentation to the council. I'm not asking you to finger anyone, but do you know of people besides your aunt and uncle who might be angry with the city for underfunding the health center?"

"I don't know about underfunded stuff, but my aunt and uncle believe Mr. Dingle did things like not get paperwork someplace on time so the city didn't have to use money to get money." He scowled. "From Uncle Sam, I think. It's not like it was Dingle's money."

Elizabeth had been taking him in by turning her head just enough to see his expression. Resentment, anger. "It must have been hard to have to push Mr. Dingle's gurney."

"Nah. You know what it's like here on Saturday nights around homecoming, or St. Patrick's Day. People come in after drinking too much, or whatever, and you have to make sure they don't barf on you." Hicks reddened. "S'cuse me."

"We use similar phrases at the police station," Elizabeth said, dryly.

He turned his head and grinned. "Sometimes they go from us to you." He sobered. "Anyway, when you see that person somewhere else later, you try not to think about the barf. They tell us that in training. So, with Dingle, I hate him, but in here, he's just a patient."

Elizabeth hesitated. "Sounds as if you have a right to be angry."

"My aunt's right about my uncle's foot. Maybe it could have been saved if he'd had help sooner. Makes me mad they can't afford to go to a regular doctor."

"Did you hear anyone else talk about being angry that the city didn't...fulfill its obligations with the health center?"

"Everybody gripes in that waiting room. You should maybe ask my aunt."

"Did Dingle talk much to you?"

"Funny you should ask. He mentioned "the bitches" a couple of times. But people say funny things when they've been put to sleep." He paused. "He woke up more when we moved him to his bed. They do lots of times."

"Any more about the women he didn't like? Or did he say who they were?"

"Nope. When we were done moving him, he got this real official voice and said, 'thank you very much young man.' Like we were in his office."

"I didn't realize he was that awake."

Hicks shrugged. "I don't know if he was."

A man's voice came from down the hall. "Got one for you, Hicks."

He turned and started toward the nurse's station. "Talk to my aunt."

"I'll do that." Since her purpose had been to assess Hicks herself, Elizabeth didn't plan to call Margaret Turner.

Elizabeth left the hospital. She'd gone there to gauge Hicks' attitude, and didn't see a level of bitterness to indicate murder. The trip had been worth it though. How many bitches were in Donald Dingle's life?

CHAPTER FOURTEEN

ELIZABETH'S *LOGLAND PRESS* STILL had not been delivered when she left for work Friday morning. She didn't like getting to the station without seeing it and didn't have time to crank up her computer to read it online.

She stopped behind a school bus picking up its middle school cargo. All the kids had on heavy sweatshirts or lighter weight jackets. Spring continued to be fickle. Tomorrow would be even cooler.

Three boys at the end of the line would be the last to board. The tallest turned to the shortest and shoved him in the shoulder. The shoved boy almost fell on his butt.

Elizabeth tapped the Crown Vic's horn, and all three boys turned. The shover's mouth dropped open and he stood still.

Elizabeth could imagine he envisioned a week of detention and angry parents. She hoped they would be angry. But she wasn't about to get into it with middle schoolers. Instead, she pointed to the bus and gestured that they should get on.

The boys moved quickly, and the bus pulled away a few seconds after they boarded.

"I wish they were all that easy," she muttered.

She entered by the station's side door, which put her in the back hall, near the locker and break rooms. From the bullpen, Hammer called, "That you, Chief?"

She walked toward her office. "It is. What's up?"

"Paper's on your desk."

When Hammer said no more, she called, "That bad?"

"Yep." He came to the doorway between the bullpen and hallway. "Makes us and the hospital look bad."

"Equal opportunity reporting." Elizabeth entered her office and took off her jacket. Hammer had left the paper folded to the article and she picked it up.

Where to Go for Health Help

Logland residents have been asking a lot of questions about how a reasonably healthy man could enter the hospital to have stents implanted and be dead a short time later.

That was the experience of the late Donald Dingle, former city clerk, who died on Tuesday. (See his obituary, page 5.)

Dr. Srini Prasad implanted two stents following Dingle's collapse at City Hall. The surgery appeared to have gone well, but Dingle died shortly after being moved to a hospital room. A shaken Mayor Sharon Humphrey said she entered his room just before Dingle's passing.

While deaths after a surgery can happen, they are rare after a procedure as common as stent implantation. An autopsy conducted by Dr. Fiona Curran of Carlinville revealed that Dingle had a large amount of ethyl alcohol in his blood, in the form of vodka.

According to those near Dingle before his collapse, he had not been drinking any kind of liquor or beer; in fact, he drank rarely. Given the amount of vodka in his blood, police are operating under the assumption that an unknown individual injected Dingle with vodka, likely through a vein.

Elizabeth raised her eyes from the paper. "Have we made a statement about that?"

Hammer shook his head. "Do we 100 percent even know that?"

Elizabeth shrugged. "We should get the initial autopsy report today. I asked Dr. Curran if the vodka could have been put in an arm or something. She said she was going to check for injection sites, but she sounded as if she discounted that idea."

"Keep reading," Hammer said.

A hospital source, who is not authorized to speak on this matter but has direct knowledge, said that injecting alcohol can easily be fatal because the body has no time to process it. Specifically, the liver does most of the work and can process about half-an-ounce per hour (roughly the amount in one ounce of 100-proof alcohol.) The body eliminates the alcohol over several hours.

Injected alcohol is in the bloodstream immediately, making a person feel drunk almost at once. While the alcohol fairly quickly disseminates into the water and fat of the body, which reduces the concentration, there is a brief time when the concentration may be toxic, even fatal. Anyone could die from injecting alcohol, but an elderly person could succumb more quickly.

Hammer shuffled his feet. "Skelly you think?"

"I'd be surprised. He'd lose everything if he talked to Pew and got found out."

Hospital officials declined an interview, but did say they are rigorously examining the cause of Dingle's death. The Logland Press asked how the hospital can ensure patient safety if they aren't sure how their safety protocols failed in the case of Donald Dingle.

CEO Harold Hargrove said, "Logland Memorial Hospital will issue a complete statement as substantive results of its quality review become available."

Mrs. Shelly Rickford of Logland contacted the Press yesterday to see what our reporters had learned.

Final Operation

Elizabeth shook her head. "Our reporters?"

Hammer snorted.

She was scheduled to have an angiogram (the procedure that examines whether any arteries near the heart are partially or fully blocked) at the end of this week. She has canceled that appointment and says she is "doctor shopping up in Springfield." She is not alone.

Samuel Goldberg of Taylorville had planned to have his right knee replaced at Logland Memorial next week. "I like my doctor, and my daughter had my grandson right here in town. But until somebody can tell me what in the hell is going on, I don't want any surgery at the hospital." Goldberg has postponed his surgery, and may go to St. Louis if "something isn't fixed fast."

Logland Press staff have heard other such comments. At a Rotary Club lunch yesterday, several members expressed concern that worries about hospital care could make it hard for businesses to attract new workers to town.

Questions to the local police have been met with little information. Chief Friedman has indicated that they have interviewed many individuals and worked with hospital security to review camera footage.

Elizabeth slapped the paper on her desk. "He hasn't talked to me for more than twenty-four hours."

Hammer cleared his throat. "I sent him a response yesterday. Pretty much what he wrote. I always tell him they come from you."

She reread the last paragraph. "I wouldn't have told him more. I wonder why he doesn't have a quote from Watson at the hospital?"

"I heard Hargrove put out the word that anyone who talks to papers or TV gets canned."

WHEN ELIZABETH MET WITH CALDERONE and Mahan in her office in late morning, she could tell they were as frustrated as she felt. "We've barely left square one." She looked at notes she'd scribbled yesterday. "What about that door near X-ray? Mahan, was it easy for someone without a badge to get through to that hallway that leads to the ER?"

"A couple times someone let in a colleague, obviously someone they knew. I suppose from a security standpoint you couldn't go back and see who got in because the second person didn't use their badge. But definitely no strangers. I'll keep an eye on it now and again."

She turned to Calderone. "How about staff from the Cardiac Cath Lab?"

"I don't know if I asked all the right questions about the heart part, but they did say he was never alone with just one staff member."

"Doesn't sound right. Norton worked on him pretty much solo in the Recovery Room," Elizabeth said.

Calderone nodded. "I think they meant when he was in the Cath Lab."

Mahan grinned. "How insulted were they that you had to ask them if they bumped him off?"

"Not too bad," Calderone said. "One of the nurses said anytime someone dies there are a lot of questions. Internal hospital investigation, not usually police." He looked at his notes. "She did say patients they work on aren't all the way asleep. Sometimes the cardiologist even talks to them."

"Talks to them?" Elizabeth said. "About what?"

"I asked that," he said. "They might tell you to hold your breath or turn your head so they can view the little catheter thing better. Heck, sometimes the doc lets people watch it all on a monitor. I did when I had mine. Don't remember much of it, though."

"I think I'm gonna throw up," Mahan said.

"Use my trash can," Elizabeth said. "So the cardiac staff think he was fine when he left them."

"They said he told them he was tired, but his color was better than when he came in."

"Either of you talk to Watson in security?"

Mahan said, "He walked by the training room when I was interviewing a nurse who worked on Dingle in the ER."

"I talked to Watson," Calderone said, "but I forgot to ask your question about where his staff were after Norton made her public accusation in the lobby."

Mahan grunted. "I know. Looking for her and the mayor. They didn't get down to autopsy until after the chief and the nurse took the elevator upstairs. Then Dr. Prasad had some questions for them about keeping people out of autopsy. They explained some stuff to him."

"Did Watson have anything else for us?

"No, and he's gone over the security tapes a lot himself. He said he even went to the city website and found pictures of a lot of staff. None he recognized."

Elizabeth smiled. "Interesting how people assume it would have to be someone who worked with him at City Hall when access would have been at the hospital."

Hammer came in and tossed a sealed envelope on Elizabeth's desk. "Preliminary autopsy report." He leaned against the door jamb.

Elizabeth took a letter opener from the center drawer of her desk and slit the seal. She scanned the summary page and tossed the report to Calderone. "Nothing we hadn't known or surmised. Specifics on the concentration of ethyl alcohol in his blood, affirmation that it essentially caused his breathing and pulse to slow until they stopped."

Calderone scanned the cover page and passed it to Mahan. "But he never vomited. Don't they usually do that?"

Hammer spoke from the doorway. "Alcohol never went to his stomach. His liver, maybe."

"If it got there." Elizabeth gestured at the report. "Where was the alcohol inserted?"

Mahan turned a page and read aloud, "Inserted directly into the vein through the existing IV line."

Elizabeth reached for it. "It says 'using a needleless port.' So the killer didn't need a needle, just a syringe?"

"Those suckers come without needles?" Mahan asked.

"You can tell you don't have kids," Hammer said. "If you have to give liquid meds to a kid they give you a syringe."

Mahan's eyebrows went up. "Oh. Or to feed a kitten."

"You volunteer at the animal shelter?" Calderone asked.

"My niece found one…" Mahan began.

"Gentleman." The three of them looked at her. "It's established you don't need a needle. Our safety instructions have taught us how to remove a needle from a syringe that has one."

Calderone stood. "Well, there's only two pharmacies in town. I'll see if they remember anyone buying the kind of syringes without needles the morning Dingle was killed."

Hammer turned to go back to his desk. "Take Mahan. He can buy kitty syringes."

CHAPTER FIFTEEN

ELIZABETH BELIEVED THE MURDERER came from City Hall, but had no direct evidence. Her gut said that you can only put people down and insult them for so long before someone either slugs you or gets back at you in a more underhanded fashion.

Her cell phone buzzed and she saw Mahan's name. He'd split from Calderone and tried to trace Floyd Yeltsin's activities. "What do you know?"

"Yeltsin's primary job is as a clerk in that small liquor store three blocks from the town square. Judging from the people who go in and out of there, he'd have lots of time to collect money or pass on whatever he wanted to sell."

"Can you talk to him while he's at work?"

"Sure, but I'd like Hammer or Calderone with me."

"We can do without Hammer for a few minutes." She hung up and went to his desk. "How do you feel about being unchained from your desk for an hour or so?" Elizabeth explained where Mahan was. "I'm hoping when he knows we have his fingerprint on Dodd's briefcase it'll make him talk more."

Hammer stood. "You think he's behind all the car break-ins?"

"Likely. What I'm most interested in is whether he'll admit to Dodd's. Then we can ask him about the insulin and syringes."

"Gotcha. I'll transfer the internal phones to you. The 9-1-1 calls will still go to county dispatch."

Elizabeth hated to have the phones. Sometimes it seemed as if Jerry Pew kept tabs on the other officers and when he saw Hammer on the street he'd call just to see if she answered. They really needed to be able to hire an admin assistant.

After a call about a roaming dog and two asking if they found Dingle's killer, Mahan called. "Yeltsin wants to trade what he says is information we want for a pass on the briefcase."

"Just the briefcase, not the other car break-ins?"

"That's what the genius says."

"Sure. Tell him we won't arrest him on that." She hung up. The phone rang immediately.

"Chief, Jerry Pew here. Saw a couple of your guys go into the liquor store. Anything I should know?"

"Aren't you supposed to do your own legwork?"

"You're a lot younger than me," he said.

"Nothing at the liquor store. We want to see if one of the employees can help us with something else. Just talked to Mahan. Not sure he can, but always worth a shot."

"Anything related to our late city clerk?"

"Nope. Very mundane." That was a sure way to derail any interest Jerry might have.

Twenty minutes later Mahan and Hammer returned and she stepped into the bullpen to greet them. "We mighta got lucky," Mahan said.

Hammer sat behind his desk. "We definitely did."

Mahan imitated a jump shot into the trash can. "Yeltsin says he sometimes provides supplies to people. Wouldn't say what kind. He says he could get fired if he says what people buy, and it's hard to get work.

"Gee," Elizabeth said, "I wonder why?"

Mahan grinned. "Anyway, Yeltsin had a call the morning Dingle died."

"What kind of call? For vodka?"

"That's what we thought," Hammer says. "Turns out he sells a lot of booze to Weeks, and Weeks asked for help getting something else. He wanted to know if Yeltsin had access to any syringes. He didn't say what for," Hammer added.

"And Yeltsin had some?" Elizabeth asked.

"He had two. He got them from the briefcase. Oh, and he gave one vial of the insulin to his mother." Hammer shook his head. "He said he left one in in the case because somebody else might really need it. We had to promise not to tell anyone he took the insulin."

Elizabeth rolled her eyes.

"She's put up with a lot from him," Mahan said. "Don't see why we need to mention it anywhere."

"We'll see," Elizabeth said. "He just happened to have the syringes on him?"

"In his work locker," Mahan said. "He thought there might be a business opportunity."

"Keep going."

Hammer grinned. "There's that sub shop a block from the liquor store. Yeltsin said he could meet Weeks there on his lunch break, but Weeks told him to go buy a breakfast sandwich."

The front door to the station opened and a women in gardening clothes came in, leading a dog around whose neck she had loosely tied a piece of rope. "Chief Friedman, this is the dog I called you about."

Elizabeth walked to the public side of the counter while Hammer reached into his desk drawer and pulled out a dog collar and short leash.

The woman noted the leash. "My, you do come prepared, don't you?"

Elizabeth took the rope, which was accompanied by several long licks to her hand from the seemingly happy part-retriever. "County folks have animal control, but we often get local pets and try to match them to owners."

The woman nodded. "I'm Melba Greene. He came right up to me and I gave him some water. He must have gotten out of a yard."

Hammer stooped down to fasten the collar on the dog. He was rewarded with several face slurps. "I'm sure we'll get a call when school's out or someone gets home from work and finds him gone."

"Thank you." Melba turned toward the door, but stopped. "I won't have any peppers or squash for a while, but I'll bring you some."

"I have a big garden," Hammer said.

Elizabeth smiled. "I don't. But don't feel obligated."

With a final wave Melba left.

Elizabeth walked behind the counter with Hammer. "I know we've had calls like this many times, but I don't recall a dog in the station."

"Rare," Hammer said. He reached into the drawer that had held the leash and took out two small dog biscuits, and grinned. "Other duties as assigned." He pointed under his desk and the dog moved there to get his biscuits. He settled happily at Hammer's feet.

Elizabeth sat on the edge of Hammer's desk. "Back to business. Yeltsin met Weeks and gave him the syringes?"

"Yep," Mahan said. "Weeks wanted one with a needle and one without, so Yeltsin used a pair of plyers from the liquor store toolbox to snap off one needle. He tossed it."

"So," Elizabeth said. "We have the mayor at the hospital, Weeks with the implement she needs to off Dingle. How does he get the syringe to her?" She nodded to Mahan. "You watched all those tapes. Did you see Weeks anywhere?"

Mahan shook his head. "I'll look again, but I'd be 99 percent positive no. He's a big guy, and he doesn't dress rough, but he wears those green work pants you can get at Wal-Mart. Not what you see in a hospital a lot."

Elizabeth sighed. "Yeltsin won't be a terribly credible witness, but maybe the sub shop has cameras."

The phone rang and Hammer picked it up, listened, and said, "Come on back. We figured it out." He gave Mahan a thumbs up. "We're one up on Calderone. That was him saying the pharmacies don't have records of selling any syringes the day Dingle was killed."

SINCE IT HAD BEEN LATE Friday when they'd learned about the syringes, Elizabeth wanted to wait to question Weeks again until they interviewed the sub shop owner and learned whether Weeks was at the hospital the day Dingle died. She assumed he'd managed to get syringes to Mayor Humphrey, and either he or Humphrey had the vodka.

Elizabeth didn't expect either of them would kill again over the weekend. She had figured she would see both of them at Dingle's Saturday memorial service, and ended up walking into the funeral home not far behind Humphrey.

Dingle's service did not tax the capacity of Leaving the Farm Funeral Home. Funeral Director Gretchen had scheduled it for the largest room, which could seat seventy, albeit close together. Elizabeth had contributed to a spray of flowers from city employees, and counted only four others.

Fewer than forty people mingled and listened to the memorial service led by Gretchen herself. Dingle's instructions said he wanted no religious observance and "no speeches from any city officials." Elizabeth only knew this because Gretchen opened the service by saying why she was leading it.

Gretchen's talk sounded more like a professional biography for a job application. She said nothing more than was in the obituary. Until she read it in the paper, Elizabeth hadn't realized Dingle's entire career had been in Logland, which was only thirty miles from the farm he'd been raised on.

Elizabeth sat in the back and let her mind wander. Dingle must have known how unpopular he was, and apparently didn't care. He certainly never behaved in a fashion to endear himself to those around him.

The only thing Elizabeth knew beyond his public persona was that Norma Norton's mother had rejected him. That had to be forty years ago or more. A person couldn't stay bitter that long, could they?

If anything, Dingle met part of the definition of a sociopath. He manipulated people and didn't seem to have an ounce of empathy for anyone. He didn't have any superficial charm, but definitely had a grandiose sense of self. None of that mattered now. As the wooden box of his cremated remains made clear, he had returned to dust.

As she studied the backs of the other attendees, Elizabeth realized that almost all of them were city employees. The paving contractor who did a lot of work for the city was there with his wife. He would have dealt a lot with Dingle and probably endured as many criticisms as Weeks did. Still, he probably made much of his living from city work.

When the service ended, attendees simply spoke briefly to each other, if at all, and left. No one had prepared an after-service meal, and it didn't appear people were going out for coffee to share memories, or whatever.

As she unlocked her car, it occurred to Elizabeth that this would be a perfect time to visit Dingle's house. She swung by the office to read Taylor's notes on the visit – which he'd finally finished – and pick up a key. The attorney who prepared Dingle's will had said police could keep it for a few days.

Taylor had Saturday duty and sat at Hammer's desk. "Hey Chief. Did anyone stand up at the funeral and confess?"

The lanky redhead had his feet on Hammer's desk and she raised an eyebrow in his direction. "If they did I didn't hear them."

Taylor put his feet on the floor and sat up straighter.

"I thought I'd stop by Dingle's place. Didn't look as if you thought anything was out of place."

"Ha. It'd be hard to be in disarray. He barely had anything."

"What do you mean?"

"I mean there was furniture in every room, a television in the living room, and a few books. No pictures of family and friends, no letters in a desk drawer. And his closet was organized by color." Taylor said this last point as if nothing could be stranger.

Elizabeth smiled. "How do you arrange yours?"

He shrugged. "I don't. I try to set an example for my kids by not throwing dirty clothes on the floor."

She nodded at Hammer's desk. "Hand me the key to the big file cabinet in the copy room, would you? I think that's where Hammer put Dingle's house key."

Taylor retrieved the key from the same drawer from which Hammer had taken the dog leash yesterday. "It is."

"What happened to the dog?"

Taylor grinned. "I saw Hammer and his wife and kids taking it for a walk this morning."

Elizabeth didn't bother printing out Taylor's notes. His verbal explanations were always better. She drove to Dingle's thinking she actually looked forward to an afternoon of laundry and cleaning, which she hadn't had time to do all week.

Dingle's small bungalow sat about two blocks behind City Hall. He could've walked on good days, but she knew he didn't. She climbed the three cement steps and inserted the key in the wood door. It opened easily.

The interior was as Taylor described it. The furniture looked expensive – solid wood end tables and a very formal sofa. She opened each kitchen cabinet, marveling at how precisely dishes – even canned food – were arranged.

After searching each drawer in his bureau and finding them similarly in order, she began to realize that she was in the home of someone who was probably severely obsessive-compulsive. Maybe that had something to do with why he was so particular about how things were done at work. Didn't explain why he had to be a prick about it.

The small room Dingle used for his office had a medium sized wooden desk with glass on the wood to protect it. The only other items were his desk chair, a recliner, and a second, smaller television, which had a DVD player. Shelves lined the walls, with cabinets underneath. The shelves held nothing decorative, in fact all the top ones were empty. Those with books were only half full.

She opened the cabinets under the shelves, knelt on the floor, and said, "Aha." Dozens, probably hundreds, of DVDs were neatly arranged. She felt like a voyeur, but pulled out a few to examine. Then more. Every movie was upbeat, many with a holiday theme.

It had never occurred to her that he would have any movies, much less that all would be those such as *The Sound of Music*, *It's a Wonderful Life*, and *The Wizard of Oz*. Most were old, but the collection included *Little Miss Sunshine* and *Mrs. Doubtfire*. *Grand Canyon* was hardly cheerful throughout, but the ending was peaceful.

Stumped, Elizabeth sat on the recliner and let her eyes travel the room. Everything perfectly organized in a contained space. The remote sat on the arm of the recliner, so once he was settled he was in control of his world. A bitter old man trying to travel to the kind of world he wanted to live in?

She shook her head. "You're not a psychologist." But Elizabeth thought she was right. Donald Dingle didn't just want things his way, he *needed* them to be just as he wanted them. And it crippled his ability to get along with anyone.

CHAPTER SIXTEEN

THE MESSAGE ON HER voice mail the following Monday was clear, though the low voice sounded disguised. "You're looking in the wrong place."

"Hey, Hammer. Come listen to this, would you?"

His chair scraped as he stood from his desk. "Sure thing, Chief." He came into her office carrying a partially open envelope.

"Mail already?"

"In the drop-off box," Hammer said.

Elizabeth pointed to her phone and redialed the code to her voice mail. The voice repeated, "You're looking in the wrong place."

"Man or woman, you think?" she asked.

He stared at the phone for a few seconds. "Sounds like a woman who's deepened her voice. A lot."

"I think so, too. The time stamp says it came through about five this morning. I assume you weren't here then."

"No, but, I think…"

"People can only put messages directly into my voice mail if they know the specific extension. And I don't give it out."

Elizabeth gestured to a chair across from her desk.

Hammer sat as he ticked off names on his fingers. "Only the mayor, Skelly, Calderone, Mahan, and me have the code."

"Right. Everything goes into the main voice mail so whoever needs to listen can pull messages."

"Unless I answer a call and put them in your voice mail."

Elizabeth nodded. "We can't be sure it's about Dingle's murder. But if you add having my code to the fact that we've been most visible looking at the hospital, it makes sense someone could want to direct us to City Hall."

"The mayor knows she's the only city official who has your extension number," Hammer said. "Why would she use it?"

Elizabeth shrugged. "Maybe she keeps it in a drawer or under her desk blotter and someone else found it."

Hammer shook his head. "You don't really believe that, do you?"

"She's only left me a direct message two or three times, and she didn't choose the code. She might need to look it up. I've seen her pull notes from under her blotter."

"Now what?" Hammer asked.

Calderone stood in the doorway. "What are we now-whatting?"

Elizabeth replayed the phone message and said why she thought it could point to someone who worked with Dingle.

Calderone frowned. "Despite accusing Skelly with no evidence, the mayor's a smart woman."

"We can't trace a voice mail," Elizabeth said, "but can the phone company give us a list of any calls that came in about that time?"

"Yep." Hammer grinned as he finished opening the envelope he'd brought with him. "Unless the caller knew how to override the time stamp, which they wouldn't. No one else will have called at 5 AM."

"Burner phone with no caller ID, don't you think?" Calderone asked.

Elizabeth nodded. "I suppose. What do…"

Final Operation

Hammer swore. "I can't believe this!" By its corner, he held an eight-and-a-half by eleven piece of copy paper that had words pasted to it.

Elizabeth pulled an evidence bag from her drawer and opened it for him. Hammer slid the paper into it.

Calderone leaned over. "What's it say?"

Elizabeth studied the note, now in its clear plastic evidence bag. *Look in the dumpster behind City Hall.* Mahan came in and she passed him the bag.

He shook his head. "When's the last time you heard of someone cutting letters out of a magazine to write a note?"

"I've never seen one," Elizabeth said. "For real, I mean. Seems like just more chances to leave fingerprints."

Calderone regarded the evidence bag for several seconds. "The only thing I can think to look for is the syringe."

"And maybe something that used to hold vodka," Mahan said.

"And perhaps a burner phone." Elizabeth told Mahan about the phone message. "Seems like someone wants to be sure we look at City Hall rather than the hospital."

Hammer shook his head. "Could be a prank. Somebody wants to see the police dig through garbage."

Elizabeth leaned against her desk. "Sure. But any evidence is meaningless unless it has fingerprints." She raised her hands in mock surrender. "Either a prank or someone's trying to have us look at the mayor or someone else in City Hall instead of maybe the real killer."

Hammer leaned against the door jamb. "Dingle was killed on a Tuesday. Garbage at City Hall gets emptied once a week, same as here, on Tuesday. Would have been picked up before Dingle died."

"So, it'll be picked up tomorrow, early," Calderone said.

Elizabeth sighed. "I guess we have to check it."

Calderone said, "I have an idea. Maybe not the best one."

"Speak now or forever holster your weapon," Elizabeth said.

"Let's send notes to a few people in City Hall. Maybe saying…let's see."

"Something that's a hint without specifics," Hammer said. "Maybe, 'Have you checked your trash today?' Something simple."

Elizabeth nodded slowly. "It'll seem nonsensical to everyone except the killer. Maybe send it to all the department heads."

"And the mayor," Hammer said.

"We're focusing on her because she was with him at the hospital. Maybe someone got to him earlier," Calderone said.

"I think he'd know if someone in the office stuck a needle in him," Elizabeth said.

Hammer shrugged. "He stuck daggers in lots of backs and people never knew."

ELIZABETH PLANNED A TWENTY-MINUTE break on Monday to pick up a sandwich at the Bully Pulpit, intending to eat it at the station. She paused at the door of the diner to read a lost dog sign, then removed it to give to Hammer. If his family wanted a dog, he'd have to go to the shelter.

Marti was in a conversational mood. "You know what's funny, Chief?"

Elizabeth handed her a ten-dollar bill. "What's that?"

"People are worried that there could be a killer at the hospital. But nobody seems scared, or even upset, about Mr. Dingle's death."

"I guess he didn't have a lot of personal friends."

"He didn't come in here a lot, but any time he did, he acted like we served dog meat."

Elizabeth smiled. "I think he put down most people and things. Would you say people are scared to go to the hospital?"

Marti shrugged. "I think mostly if they might have to stay overnight. But there's a lot of talk. Plus, anyone who knows Skelly likes him. People think it's unfair he's still off work when you guys don't seem to suspect him of anything."

As she accepted her change and put a dollar on the counter as a tip, Elizabeth thought Skelly may have been right. Fear could make some people go to other towns for procedures they'd normally use Logland Memorial for. She didn't know a lot about how hospitals balanced their books, but she figured a small hospital like Logland's couldn't afford to lose many patients.

When she turned toward the door, Elizabeth had another thought. "Who was Mr. Dingle with when he came here to eat?"

Marti grinned. "Mr. Gangle and sometimes the budget director woman. She lost a bet with Gangle a couple times, so she had to eat with Dingle."

Elizabeth placed her sandwich on her desk but had not taken a bite when the intercom buzzed. Hammer said, "Mayor called some kind of emergency council work session tonight. Apparently some budget numbers were miscalculated, and they're supposed to take a vote on the budget in a couple of days."

"Huh. That would certainly give the mayor a reason to be in the building late."

"Yep. Stay later than the others and search the dumpster."

"Very crafty." Elizabeth opened the sandwich wrapping. *Too crafty?*

SHE DIDN'T USUALLY ATTEND budget work sessions. Elizabeth submitted the Police Department's funding request with a binder of background material. If a council member had questions, they usually called.

Department heads had a standing invitation to council work sessions, unless the mayor or a council member asked that it be closed. When she walked into that night's meeting, Mayor Humphrey's eyebrows shot up. Elizabeth figured half of the reason was because she didn't usually attend any meetings in jeans and a Logland PD sweat shirt.

Her eyes swept the room. Council members sat at the table. The only department heads present were Weeks and Franz, and she would have to be at a meeting about the budget.

Adrian Gangle made no attempt to hide his irritation. "Why are you here, Chief Friedman?"

She smiled as she sat with the other staff along the wall of the fifteen-by-fifteen conference room. "I heard some numbers might need to be rejiggered, and after the discussion at the last full council meeting, I thought I'd make myself available in case you had any questions about proposed police expenditures."

A woman said, "Thank you, Chief."

Elizabeth nodded at Maxine Minder. Rarely did the retired teacher say anything unless the topic dealt with the Recreation Department or Head Start Programs. Elizabeth took the comment as support for the police.

"Yes," Humphrey said, "thanks. I called this meeting because Ms. Franz notified me that the salary we had recommended for a pediatric physician assistant at the community health center appears so low it would affect recruitment." Humphrey nodded at Franz.

The budget director opened a large, black binder. "I checked the numbers Dorothy Washington provided yesterday against ads for similar jobs at hospitals and clinics near us. Most of those were $10 to $25,000 more than we'd planned. I don't think that's an amount we can absorb without making cuts elsewhere."

Elizabeth sat through almost thirty minutes of sometimes heated discussion. She didn't understand why no one from the health center had been asked to appear, but it was hardly her problem.

When the discussion seemed to be at an impasse, she said, "We may have at least one retirement coming up this year. The replacement officer would have a lower salary than a more senior one. You could take $2,500 out of the Police Department budget."

It wasn't an offer that would cost the department anything. Bottom line, if the police budget ran short it would mean there'd been an emergency, and the council always managed to find money for dire circumstances. Which were mostly overtime for weather emergencies, if at all.

"Thank you, Chief," Humphrey said.

Final Operation

Weeks cleared his throat. "I almost feel bad saying this, but we won't have a city clerk for a while. Won't you save some money there?"

"Possibly," Humphrey said. She surveyed the other council members. "I think Patricia was correct to call the need for added funds to our attention, especially since the final vote on the budget is in a few days. But my sense is we can move the $2,500 Chief Friedman will relinquish and watch for other savings later."

Elizabeth saw Weeks flush. His suggestion would probably save a lot more than hers, but Humphrey hadn't credited him.

After another ten minutes, the work session disbanded. Elizabeth stood when the others did, and had reached the door when Humphrey called to her.

She stood aside so Maxine Minder and Adrian Gangle could leave, and then faced the mayor. "Ma'am?"

Humphrey stuck pencils in her purse and tucked a binder under her arm. "Thanks for volunteering some funds."

Elizabeth shrugged slightly. "My bank account will not decrease."

The mayor glanced at the door of the now-empty room. "Sorry to spoil your evening."

Elizabeth sensed she wanted to say something else, so she waited.

Finally Humphrey met her eyes. "I'm sorry about how I handled that situation with Skelly, Dr. Hutton. I feel as if I've damaged our good relationship."

Damaged? How about destroyed? "It was...not a good day, but I'm sure we'll move beyond it." *Why is she talking to me about this now?*

"How is Skelly doing?"

Elizabeth chose her words carefully. "He'll be better when the hospital comes to its senses and puts him back on duty."

"Would it help if I called someone?"

"I think they have to finish their review, and then everything will play out." Elizabeth moved toward the door again. "If you don't mind, I'm on call tonight. I want to get some shut-eye."

"Of course."

Elizabeth stepped into the hall and made for a side door. She definitely didn't want the mayor to know she had no plans to go home right away.

CHAPTER SEVENTEEN

THE LIGHTS IN CITY HALL had gone out quickly. Elizabeth knelt on the asphalt near the rear entrance, hidden behind Calderone's SUV, and alert to her surroundings. City Hall backed into an alley, but a fence at the perimeter denied access to the narrow passage. Ten parking spaces surrounded the aging dumpster, but none close enough for a car to get banged by the industrial garbage truck that came weekly.

The sound of something like a soft food wrapper being balled up reached her. The lights at the back of the building created shadows, but no one appeared from them. The sound came again. She whispered to herself, "Ugh, rats."

Her knees ached from stooping beside the SUV. No matter how much she ached, she didn't want to stand to stretch her legs.

Elizabeth's thoughts turned to the note that said to search the dumpster. Maybe a prankster was close by, taking delight that a few officers were hanging around City Hall's parking lot. She hoped they weren't wasting time. Or the overtime budget.

The anonymous email Hammer had sent to several City Hall officials had not generated calls to the station, or even any discernible interest. She still didn't believe she would see the mayor exit the building to search the garbage.

After another ten minutes, she began to relax. The note the police received had been a crank's ploy.

They would soon know if anyone wanted to check the garbage. Pick-up at City Hall would be at seven AM tomorrow. If the mayor, or anyone else, were to search the dumpster, it would have to be tonight. If no one showed up, Elizabeth would have to decide whether to remove most of the garbage bags. They'd probably have to use the jail cells to spread out all the trash.

She texted Calderone. "You think she's coming?"

His reply: "Let's wait ten more."

Elizabeth responded: "Your knees aren't on the pavement."

Calderone texted back a frown face.

She grimaced to herself and shifted her weight. She'd been furious at Mayor Humphrey for falsely accusing Skelly of killing Donald Dingle. Still, it seemed impossible that Mayor Humphrey had joined Nurse Norton in trying to implicate Skelly.

In fact, if Humphrey had killed Dingle, she hadn't planned it. Or at least not the timing. How would she know Dingle would have a heart attack? Or had she given him something to provoke it, and added a vodka injection when the attack didn't kill him? It would be weeks before they had the full toxicology report.

And was being near Nurse Norton when the woman accused Skelly just dumb luck? Or bad luck? If Humphrey had killed Dingle, Humphrey would have been better off not involving herself in any aspect of the post-crime activities. But not all amateur killers thought rationally.

No, it didn't make sense that Mayor Humphrey killed her city clerk. Wanted to, maybe.

City Hall's steel exit door opened with a loud creak. Elizabeth cursed to herself. She faced the full length of the back of the door, not the side that would clearly show who was about to come down the short flight of stairs.

She peered around the SUV's tire. A woman, head covered in a flowing scarf and wearing a long raincoat, turned her head left and right. The scarf shrouded each side of her face, so

Elizabeth still couldn't identify her. She carried no purse or other bag.

Apparently convinced she was alone in back of City Hall, the woman walked swiftly to the large commercial dumpster. Elizabeth's heart quickened.

The woman pulled a small flashlight from a pocket and shined it around the dumpster. The thin light bounced over the narrow strip of concrete behind the dumpster, then swept the weeds behind the concrete, then moved toward the closed lid.

Silently Elizabeth stood and walked toward the bin. Surprise would work to her advantage, so she spoke loudly. "Ma'am, what are you looking for?"

The scarf fell from the woman's head, and Patricia Franz jumped and swirled toward Elizabeth. "What? Who? Why, Chief, what are you doing here?"

Elizabeth was glad about the poor lighting. Surely shock registered on her face. "A better question might be what are you looking for?"

"Looking for? Nothing." Franz examined the ground and turned back to Elizabeth. "I was heading home and, and I heard a noise behind the dumpster. I thought someone might be hurt."

"It looked as if everyone had gone home after tonight's work session. What are you doing here?"

Franz's shoulders sagged. "Did you send me that note?"

From behind Elizabeth, Calderone said, "Actually, I wrote it. The chief couldn't believe anyone in City Hall killed Mr. Dingle."

Without looking over her shoulder, Elizabeth said, "And I'll never doubt you again, Calderone."

Elizabeth spoke to Franz. "Come toward me and put your hands behind your back."

Franz stood straighter. "It's not what you think!"

Using an even tone of voice, Elizabeth said, "Then when we get to the station you can tell us what we should think."

Calderone motioned to her and Franz walked toward him. "Hands behind your back," he said. She did so, and he positioned himself behind her to place the cuffs on her wrists.

Elizabeth walked with the two of them to his patrol car, which sat one building down from City Hall. "I'll meet you at the station in five minutes." She walked the short distance to her car on the side street. She got in and leaned her head into the headrest. *We just brought in the budget director, and I thought we might arrest the mayor.*

Even though he was close to retirement, she should probably promote Calderone to sergeant.

WHEN THEY ARRIVED AT the police station, Elizabeth took Franz to the conference room and removed her handcuffs. Franz accepted a cup of decaf coffee but would say nothing beyond thank you.

With Grayson sitting outside the door that led to the conference room, Elizabeth, Calderone, and Mahan stood in her office. "You both looked at those tapes. Was she on any?" Elizabeth asked.

Calderone shook his head as he studied a notebook. "My notes mention several people, besides patients, that I couldn't identify, but they were just folks walking in the hall."

"No women about her age even?" Mahan asked.

He flipped pages. "One about her height and maybe age. I mentioned her earlier -- wearing a ball cap. Can't tell if she had long or short hair. But she carried flowers and one of those cutesy gift shop bags. Looked like she was visiting someone."

Elizabeth pointed at Mahan. "See if Watson or someone will let you go through those security tapes again," Elizabeth said.

"At this time of night?" Mahan asked.

"No time like the present," Elizabeth said.

Mahan left and Elizabeth turned to Calderone. "You told her she could ask for a lawyer?"

"Sure. She said she didn't need one."

Elizabeth sat behind her desk and Calderone took a chair across from her. She sighed. "She probably knows we don't have anything on her beyond a late-night trip to the dumpster."

"True, but she never asked us why we were there, or if we thought she had done something wrong."

Elizabeth nodded. "I thought that, too. She's a smart woman, she knows she can't just sit there."

He nodded, slowly. "So if Mahan finds her on the security tapes, what was she doing? As far as we know, she never got near Dingle in the hospital."

"Bringing someone either a syringe or vodka."

Calderone smiled. "If she worked with Dingle every day, she probably had the vodka."

"Let's say she was bringing one of those things to the mayor. She'd be an accomplice, which could get her quite a prison sentence."

"Unless she gives us the goods on the murderer," Calderone said.

"The goods? You've been watching some old cop shows."

Calderone grinned. "It's how I get to sleep. Seriously, should we let on that we don't think she killed him, but explain how serious it is to be an accessory before the fact?"

Elizabeth rubbed her temples. "Why can't we catch more people during the day? I want to chat with our dear state's attorney. I've been meaning to call him to ask why he never called to ask about the case."

She picked up her desk phone and called the State's Attorney's office. The answering service picked up. "Chief Friedman here. I'd like to talk to Mr. Donaldson." She paused. "Yes, tonight. It's urgent." She hung up and said, "The service said it will take a few minute so get him. He'll call back."

She went to the break room to make a cup of tea while Calderone walked down the hall to see if Grayson needed a quick break. While the water heated she stared at the bulletin board announcements about a 'Spring Fling' the Chamber of Commerce planned for the next weekend, and a silent auction in three weeks, sponsored by the Hospital Auxiliary. She hoped the hospital wouldn't have to put the brakes on its volunteers' fundraising because they had fewer patients and no longer needed the planned equipment.

Franz was definitely not as worried as she should be. Who did she expect to ride in on a white horse to save her? She probably figured as long as she said nothing she couldn't be charged with anything. For now, she was perhaps correct. Elizabeth hoped Mahan found something on hospital security tapes.

Because Franz hadn't been considered a suspect, no one had questioned her whereabouts the day Dingle died. Had she been in the office from the time he left in the ambulance until he died?

She finished steeping her tea and had almost reached her office when the phone rang. She picked it up on the third ring.

Xavier Donaldson had been driving back from a family night at the movies in Springfield. "I'm going to assume this couldn't wait, Chief."

"I thought we should discuss options while a potential suspect was still upset about her first ride in a patrol car in handcuffs." Elizabeth outlined why they had watched the dumpster and described Franz's unwillingness to say why she was there.

Donaldson cleared his throat. In the background Elizabeth could hear children talking. She figured Donaldson would be less disdainful than usual.

"I hear you, Chief. Seems she would have asked what the heck you were doing back there, and demanded to know why you were interested in her. Did you Mirandize her?"

"No, though we told her she could call counsel. We were thinking of letting her know that if she didn't participate in the murder itself she could help herself by telling us if she knows who did. But I didn't want to speak for you."

"Thanks." Donaldson paused for several seconds. "She took you up on a lawyer?"

"No. She won't talk to us at all anymore. She's just sitting in the conference room."

"Huh. Well, if you explain her rights and she doesn't waive them, I see no problem in taking the path you suggested."

The path I suggested? He really doesn't want his kids to guess which case he's talking about.

"And what about timeframes?" Elizabeth asked. "Should I suggest she'd get a lesser sentence if she cooperates?"

"Yes, you can even tell her you talked to me. Just don't talk numbers."

"Sure. One more question, could be relevant. Usually you call when we have a big case. May I ask why you didn't?"

Donaldson said nothing for so long Elizabeth thought he'd disconnected.

"The mayor called. I can't recall her exact words, but I inferred you and she had talked. She said she should never have listened to the nurse who accused Dr. Hutton. Something about the heat of the moment." He paused. "I was left with the impression that you were going to call me. Just this morning I wondered why you hadn't."

"I spoke to her a lot, but only about her own actions and her interactions with Dingle. I certainly didn't suggest she should discuss anything with you."

"You think it means something?" Donaldson asked.

"In police parlance, we'd look at that call as some sort of clue. Or maybe it's nothing. Thanks for letting me know."

Elizabeth hadn't realized her palms were sweaty. Before she hung up the phone, she wiped the receiver.

CHAPTER EIGHTEEN

ELIZABETH AND CALDERONE ENTERED the conference room to proceed as she and Donaldson had discussed, but knowing the conversation could go in a very different direction.

Patricia Franz stared at them coolly and then transferred her attention to her mug of coffee.

Elizabeth sat across from her. "I know we've asked you several times if you wanted counsel. Before we speak now, I'm asking again."

Franz kept her gaze on the mug. "I have nothing to say."

Elizabeth took a small tape recorder from her pocket. She still preferred one with a tape. "You are welcome to stay silent. I will record what I say and anything you do."

Franz shrugged.

Elizabeth nodded slightly at Calderone and he turned on the recorder and noted the date and who was in the room. He continued, "You already figured out that we were waiting behind City Hall to see if someone would respond to that note we sent to several offices."

When she didn't say anything, he continued. "It seems logical that you wanted something from that dumpster, and we think it may have related to Donald Dingle's murder. We've taped off the area behind City Hall and people will search the dumpster's contents tomorrow."

Franz shifted in her seat. "Unpleasant work."

Elizabeth took over. "I've discussed your situation with State's Attorney Donaldson..."

Franz almost yelled, "My situation! I have no situation."

"And yet," Elizabeth said softly, "you've never asked why we brought you here."

Franz flushed.

"It's possible that whatever happened to Donald Dingle involved more than one person. In a situation like that, if an individual helps law enforcement, the prosecutor strongly considers that in making a sentencing recommendation." Elizabeth let that idea linger.

Franz said nothing.

"This is not a very comfortable place to spend the night," Calderone said.

"You can't keep me here!"

"We can't keep you here very long unless the State's Attorney files charges," Elizabeth said. "But you'll be our guest tonight. Since you're working late, I assume you have child care for your son."

"None of your business," Franz said.

Elizabeth stood, and Calderone followed.

They reached the door when Franz said, "Don't I get one phone call?"

Elizabeth faced her. "You can make one, two if you need to call a lawyer and let someone know where you are." She nodded toward the phone on the credenza against the wall. "I'll come back in five minutes. We won't be able to listen to your conversation, but we can see the number you call."

She and Calderone stepped into the hall, and she shut the door. In a low voice, she asked, "What do you think?"

He shrugged. "Progress, maybe."

Grayson had left a note on the doorjamb to Elizabeth's office. "Went back out on patrol."

At her desk, with Calderone facing her, Elizabeth said, "My guess is whatever she decides, she'll be with us overnight."

Calderone shook his head. "County's better set up for females."

Elizabeth nodded. "It is. Our two cells are clean and I believe Hammer recently ordered new pillows." She smiled. "But I don't think we've had a woman overnight since I came here."

"Not since," Calderone stared at the calendar on the wall behind Elizabeth, "some woman from out of town punched a guy at...what bar was that?"

Elizabeth waited a few seconds, and he finally said, "The Bees Knees. Don't ask. Anyway, I bet that was ten years ago."

"If we transfer her to county tonight, two things happen. First, it's a lot of rigmarole to talk to her tomorrow. Second, somebody over there will alert the damn press. We'll not only be flooded with calls, if she isn't the killer, it could put the person on alert."

"You think she did it?" Calderone asked.

Elizabeth shrugged. "The way Dingle treated her, I'm sure she wished him gone as much as any of us. Hard to figure out how she could do it, but she's a smart woman."

Calderone looked at the clock. "Ten minutes are up."

"Okay. Check out the cells real quick, would you?"

He grinned. "If she thinks they really suck, maybe we'll get a budget boost."

"Shut up," Elizabeth said, but smiled. "While you do that, I'll let Grayson know he and I will be in here tonight."

Calderone did a palms-up gesture. "Why would you stay here?"

"Good idea for a woman to be here with a female prisoner. And I don't want to put Grayson in the position of being alone with her."

Five minutes later, Elizabeth and Calderone entered the conference room to find Franz back in her chair. Elizabeth thought her red eyes indicated she'd been crying, but she was composed now. They sat across from her. "What did you decide, Ms. Franz?"

"I do want to consult an attorney, but it's late. He can't be down here from Decatur until morning. And I'm exhausted."

Elizabeth nodded. "We don't have many overnight guests, but I think you'd be better off with us than in county. This isn't the Ritz, but you can get some sleep."

Franz drew a breath. "I haven't eaten since lunch."

Calderone said, "We can find something."

Elizabeth said, "I'll remain in the station overnight with Officer Grayson." She stood. "I hope you decide to help yourself. I'll be back for you in a minute."

She and Calderone left the conference room and Elizabeth pointed to the back exit. "Go home."

They walked toward the far end of the hallway, which led to the very austere, cinderblock interview room and, behind it, Logland's two jail cells. Calderone said, "It's kind of hitting me that if she didn't do it, we're putting the city budget director behind bars for the night."

Elizabeth stopped at her office. "She did something, or she'd be talking to us." As she entered, her cell phone rang.

Mahan sounded excited. "Chief, remember Calderone talked about a woman in the ball cap carrying flowers? It could be Patricia Franz."

"So you aren't certain?"

"No, but the height and build are the same, and she never, and I mean never, looks up. She's shown a couple places as she goes from the lobby, past a patient hallway on two, then to the cafeteria and..."

"Second floor doesn't have the cardiac unit," Elizabeth said.

"I know, but wouldn't it be smart to meet someone on another floor to give them the stuff?"

Elizabeth rolled her eyes, glad he couldn't see it. "I suppose. So you lose her in a patient hallway?"

"Yep, but she comes back and takes the elevator down. Without the flowers. And always with her head down. Even when she passes people."

"You'd think that would attract attention," Elizabeth said. "How long was she in the patient area?"

"Not long, maybe five minutes."

"In the morning, find out which staff were on duty then and if they remember her."

"Sure," Mahan said. "And she had on what looked like dark pants and a dark blazer of some kind. You'd call her outfit nondescript. And flat shoes."

"Did they print any stills for you?"

"Night guy didn't know how. I told him the stills could wait until morning, earlier the better."

"That's fine. I just remembered Watson was going to send over digital files. I hope they aren't sitting around here. If they are, I'll owe his guys a pizza."

Elizabeth hung up. The woman's clothes were hardly the kind Franz wore at work, and this was during the work day. She could have changed somehow. Elizabeth stretched. She'd have to let her brain stop or she'd never get any sleep sitting at her desk.

TUESDAY MORNING, ELIZABETH DECLINED Hammer's suggestion that she "take a short break at the diner." She always kept a clean shirt in her desk and had freshened up in the rest room before the day shift arrived.

Thankfully, Franz hadn't asked for anything overnight, so Grayson hadn't had to wake her. Elizabeth had almost four hours of sleep.

She stood next to Hammer's desk in the bullpen. "Have you heard a peep from anyone about Franz's presence here?"

"Nothing. And Jerry Pew hasn't heard because there's nothing on the paper's website." Hammer reached into his inbox and pulled out the *Logland Press*, which had been underneath a file folder. "It's Tuesday, so good news from the paper."

Elizabeth groaned and took it. "How bad is it?"

Hammer's tone held disgust. "He doesn't jam us up too bad, but he makes it sound as if the town will die if we don't get this solved in a few days."

Elizabeth scanned the front page. Much discussion of the case dealt with Dingle's memorial service. The couple of quotes about the man talked about his 'dedication' to the city or how hard he worked. Not one word about his role in the community, nor did anyone lament his death. Adrian Gangle's brief quote talked only about having worked often with Dingle.

She glanced at Hammer. "I would be so sad to think I'd be remembered this way."

"You won't be. Go to the editorial."

Elizabeth flipped to the inside back page.

Why a Hospital Matters

A town whose hospital becomes simply a clinic loses more than medical care. In fact, the unemployment cascade would be fierce. Many hospital staff would lose their jobs, and some would move closer to work in other cities. The money hospital staff spend on services such as daycare, dry cleaning or dining out would vanish, along with those jobs.

Those are simply the immediately obvious losses. As families move, schools would have fewer students. If those selling homes so they can get to new jobs can't easily offload their houses, the average cost of homes could plummet.

Elizabeth slapped the paper on Hammer's desk. "I can't read more of Jerry's negativity." She picked up the paper again. "There's no way he wrote this. He doesn't say things like 'offload houses' or home prices 'could plummet.'"

Hammer nodded. "Yeah. I bet he had a call or email from a realtor. Okay, change of topic. Did Franz call anyone besides her lawyer?"

"I told her she could make a call this morning if she needed to check on her son. She could have done that, or maybe she left a message on the City Hall phone simply saying she'd be out today."

Hammer shrugged. "Well, we've got a couple hours until all hell breaks loose for sure. Jerry Pew checks yesterday's log about eleven every morning."

Elizabeth grimaced. "How did you word last night in the online log?"

He grinned. "Investigation of a possible prowler behind City Hall."

Elizabeth laughed aloud. "Very good. He'll ask about it, but he won't run right over."

As Elizabeth turned to go to her office, Hammer picked up the ringing phone and the front door banged as Marti came in. Spring wind had blown her hair every which way, and Elizabeth thought her frown was akin to panic.

Elizabeth went to the counter. "What's up Marti?"

"Did you see the paper? Do you really think everyone will move? Have you found Mr. Dingle's killer yet?"

Elizabeth gave her the peace sign. "Whoa. Marti, this is Jerry Pew trying to sell papers by being dramatic. The hospital isn't going anywhere, and neither are your customers."

"Hardly anyone is at breakfast. Not even Skelly."

That struck Elizabeth as odd. She didn't frequent the diner every morning but he did. He hated to cook. "

"Marti, he could have just slept in." She reached into her pocket and took out her wallet and removed a twenty dollar bill and a five. "Some of us worked really late. How about bringing us a batch of scrambled eggs and a bunch of toast?"

"I, uh."

"Should I give you more?" Elizabeth asked.

"No, but the eggs are on the house."

Elizabeth said, "Not going to happen."

Hammer said, "No way, Marti."

Marti squared her shoulders and took the twenty-five dollars. "I'm going to tell everyone you said it will all be okay." She turned and left.

Hammer cleared his throat and Elizabeth faced him. "What?"

"She isn't the only who thinks that. A reporter from Springfield just called to ask if the hospital was closing. I told her not just no but hell no, and gave her Hargrove's name for a more appropriate quote."

"What did she say?" Elizabeth asked.

"She laughed."

"I wish I could."

PATRICIA FRANZ HAD BEEN up since six Tuesday morning, and had the benefit of her comb and whatever make-up had been in her purse. Elizabeth had personally retrieved it and put it back. This would never have happened in Chicago, she thought.

Hammer had also shared some of the eggs and toast that Nick brought over. Franz responded with only two or three words whenever they said anything to her.

Her attorney drove down from Decatur and appeared at eight-thirty. Peter Urich and Franz had gone to college together and, as he told Elizabeth, kept in touch. Before he met with Franz, Elizabeth explained where they had found her and that she was being questioned about possible participation in the murder of Donald Dingle.

As she led him to the conference room, Urich began to protest the "flimsy pretext" for keeping her overnight.

Elizabeth didn't look at him as she opened the door to the room and gestured he should enter. "Maybe Ms. Franz will give you an explanation for her behavior. She's on a forty-eight hour hold. I could have arrested her for hindering a police investigation. Your advice may help preclude that."

Urich met with Franz for an hour before he left the conference room and told Hammer he and his client were ready to meet with Elizabeth. He returned to the conference room.

Elizabeth looked from Hammer to Calderone. "I say Calderone and I each carry in two mugs of coffee. Kill 'em with kindness."

Calderone yawned. "Anything to speed stuff up."

"I'll pour the mugs," Hammer said. He did, and opened the door so Elizabeth and Calderone could enter carrying a mug in each hand. Under her arm, Elizabeth had a manila folder with some of the still photos from the hospital security video.

"Thank you," Franz took the coffee.

Elizabeth realized it was the word she had spoken the most in the last ten hours. She addressed Urich. "Counselor, has your client decided to assist law enforcement in the investigation of Donald Dingle's murder?"

Franz raised her voice. "I had nothing to do with it."

Urich made a downward gesture with one palm. "We'd like to know why you believe Ms. Franz is involved in any way with this crime."

Calderone said, "Maybe we can start by having her tell us why she checked out the dumpster behind City Hall last night."

"We aren't too clear on the 'thought she heard a noise and went to check' premise," Elizabeth said, dryly.

"Well, that's all I've got, so that's all you've got," Franz snapped.

Elizabeth opened the folder and slid across the table a still shot of the woman in the ball cap at the hospital the day Dingle was murdered. "I have an officer at City Hall checking your schedule for that day. On an ordinary day, people don't remember everything. For the day the town's city clerk died, people who worked with him will recall a lot."

Lawyer and client stared at the photo. Elizabeth could imagine Franz's brain trying to find a workable angle. In fact, it might not be her. But if not, she would likely have shoved the photo back across the table immediately.

No one spoke for perhaps fifteen seconds.

When Franz met Elizabeth's gaze, her eyes watered. "All I did was bring her a small, padded envelope."

CHAPTER NINETEEN

RATHER THAN ASK WHO 'SHE' was, Elizabeth focused on the task itself. "Where were you to take the envelope?"

Franz regained some of her bluster. "To the bus stop."

Urich said, "Patricia."

"To the damn hospital!"

"And how did you get it to her? Leave it somewhere? Hand it to her?"

"Go on," Urich said.

"I went to the cafeteria and sat near her. We didn't speak. When I got up, I left the envelope on the table, under a couple of napkins."

Elizabeth made a mental note to ask Watson to look for the woman in the ball cap in the cafeteria. A bonus if she sat next to Mayor Humphrey.

Calderone shifted in his seat. "Did you see her pick it up?"

Franz nodded. "When I put a coffee cup in the trash can I glanced back. She was putting it in her purse. She carries one that's big enough to hold a couple manila folders."

Elizabeth wished Franz would say a name. It had to be Mayor Humphrey.

But Elizabeth couldn't say the name first. "How did you know to bring her an envelope?"

"She said it would be on her desk in an hour, and I should get it and bring it."

"When did she tell you this?"

"While Dingle was getting his stents put in, she came back to the office to tell us what was going on. Before she went back, she told me about the envelope and said I should bring it later."

At this point, Elizabeth didn't know for sure what was in the envelope. She felt certain that Weeks had provided one or two syringes, but thought the mayor could have supplied the vodka. At least she was in the best position to administer it.

Urich spoke. "As you can see, my client's role was minimal. Simply delivering an item from one city employee to another."

Elizabeth couldn't keep the scorn from her voice. "Gee, a lawyer who thinks an accomplice to murder was functioning like the local pizza delivery?"

Franz turned to Urich and almost shrieked. "I told you we shouldn't talk to them!" Her face red, she looked from Calderone to Elizabeth. "I'm done talking to you two."

Calmly, Elizabeth said, "Thanks I think we have what we need." She looked at Urich. "Someone from the state's attorney's office will contact you directly." She stood.

Franz had lost some of her bluster. "I get out now, right?"

"You mentioned your son when we spoke in City Hall." Elizabeth said. "You can make any phone calls needed to arrange his care." She turned to Urich. "It's up to you to see that none of her calls are to her cohorts."

Franz sat back in her chair, mouth partly open.

Elizabeth and Calderone walked quickly to her office. Hammer stayed at his desk, and she called to him. "I want to see if we can get a search warrant for Milton Weeks' desk. I've seen the wine he keeps there. Maybe he was also the source for the vodka."

"That's pretty tenuous," Hammer said.

"We also have Weeks' contact with Yeltsin at the liquor store. There could be receipts for vodka. Any receipts from the liquor store would strengthen his ties to Yeltsin."

Hammer arched his eyebrows. "You let him keep booze in his desk?"

"It was sealed. I pick my battles." She didn't add that he'd made it clear he imbibed at work.

"I'll get something started on a search warrant," Hammer said.

As she and Calderone sat, he said, "She never used the mayor's name."

"And Franz didn't talk about any syringes. But she did say that 'she' came back to City Hall when Dingle's stents were being implanted."

Elizabeth picked up the phone. "We have to hope Watson keeps good camera eyes on the hospital cafeteria."

After talking to Watson, she sent Calderone to the hospital to go through security video with his staff. She then called Donaldson. "Franz may be able to make a case that she didn't know what the mayor intended to do with what was in the envelope, but I think their clandestine method to transfer them from Franz to Humphrey makes it clear they had nefarious intent."

"Do you really think she can say she didn't know what she delivered?" Donaldson asked.

"I hope hospital security spots her in the cafeteria and we get a good view of the package. A box you might argue that she didn't know what was in it, but syringes or vodka in an envelope could be easier to spot."

Donaldson had several questions about Franz's son, but all Elizabeth could tell him was that the child was school age.

"I'm concerned her attorney will use that to ask for low bail," Donaldson said.

"Hard to run with a kid in tow," Elizabeth said. "And Urich will also argue she's a cooperating witness."

"Barely. I'll let you know…"

Elizabeth interrupted Donaldson. "I have a favor."

"What is it, Chief?"

"I'd like to go over to City Hall one more time before they know we have Franz. I think her presence here is not widely known, or our phone would be ringing off the hook."

"You've probably got an hour before I talk to a judge about a bail hearing." Donaldson hung up.

Elizabeth told Hammer where she was going and drove the few blocks to City Hall quickly. She found Carolyn Maitlin at her desk, looking professional as usual, and carefully avoiding eye contact.

Elizabeth plopped into a side chair next to Maitlin's desk. "You know what I find?"

Maitlin put down her pen. "What's that, Chief?"

"When you want to know something, you ask the admin staff. Their knowledge is in direct proportion to the distance from the bosses, and you sit pretty close to Patricia Franz and the mayor."

Maitlin flushed. "What is it you think I know?"

"I think you wanted *us* to know that something seemed off over here, in terms of Dingle's death. Maybe you weren't sure what it was. So you left me an anonymous message early yesterday morning. When no one would be in the office to answer your call."

"Why me?" she asked.

"Because the person knew the code that would put them directly into my voice mail."

"The mayor never gave me anything like that," Maitlin said, very fast.

Elizabeth nodded. "I believe you. But the other day she reached under her desk blotter to get a piece of paper she wanted me to have. Perhaps we should see what else she keeps under there."

Maitlin sat up straighter and glanced toward the far side of the office, where Heather Wilson stood at the copier, which belched paper. "I don't *know* anything. I just, well, was thinking about who was in the office the day he died. And when they stepped out."

"Such as?"

"Patricia never goes home for lunch." Quickly she added. "But that doesn't have to mean anything."

"True, but it could be a starting point for us," Elizabeth said. "Who else did something different?"

Maitlin shook her head. "No one, really. I told you the mayor came to tell us what happened before Mr. Dingle went to surgery. She isn't tied to her desk. So that's normal for her."

"Any reason to think Ms. Franz was especially angry with Dingle?"

"He was always mean to her. I don't think that day, or the day before, was any different."

A voice boomed from near the entrance to the suite. "Chief Friedman. Lots of time to lounge?"

Elizabeth turned her head slightly and took in Adrian Gangle. "No subterfuge with the college today?"

He looked toward Humphrey's closed office door and back to Elizabeth. "I don't know what you're talking about."

"Sure you do. If not, ask President Dodd for a copy of Donald Dingle's memo. You were cc'd on it, so Dodd'll probably give it to you."

Gangle stalked into the hallway and Elizabeth saw him jab the elevator button. She turned back to Maitlin.

"Anyone else up here that day who usually isn't?"

When Maitlin frowned, Elizabeth said, "On the day Dingle died."

"Oh. Well, you know, people came in and out to see what happened. Everyone saw the ambulance. Or at least heard about it."

"So, nothing unusual?"

Maitlin smiled. "Milton Weeks came up to fix the squeak in the mayor's door. He said it was probably the last direction Mr. Dingle would give him, so he should get it done."

Elizabeth told her heart not to beat so fast. "Do you remember the time?"

"Before lunch, so maybe eleven-ish."

Bingo. Hours before Dingle died, Weeks said he might not get another annoying call from the guy. If he was giving the mayor some syringes or vodka, he knew he wouldn't get another one of Dingle's orders.

AS ELIZABETH WALKED INTO her office, Skelly called from where he sat in a chair next to Hammer. "I hear you've made a lot of progress." He took a bite of a brownie from a plate on Hammer's desk.

She stopped next to Skelly and smiled. "Where did you hear that?"

"My new best friend, Nurse Norma Norton."

Elizabeth felt something like a jolt in her rib case. She had been firm with Skelly about not dating. She couldn't stand the gossip or risk losing her job. She had no right to resent his cheery attitude when talking about another woman. "How in the heck does she know anything?"

"She's friends with someone in City Hall, and it's all over the building that after you talked to Carolyn Maitlin she went in the ladies room and threw up."

"That's too bad." Elizabeth figured she felt guilty for ratting out Franz, whom she'd known for years.

"Come on, Elizabeth. Fess up."

"You first. How'd you and your accuser get to be best friends?"

"I told her we could talk about anything, and I could not repeat it if the conversation was covered by doctor-patient privilege."

"And was it?" Elizabeth asked.

"I'm an emergency room physician two days a week. We *urgently* needed to have a conversation about why she might be confused about a needle in the Recovery Room."

"But you can't tell me what you discussed?"

"Were you listening?"

"I was." When Hammer pointed at the plate, Elizabeth took a brownie.

"I'm pleased with what she told me. Your turn," Skelly said.

She took a bite and nodded at Hammer. "These are good. Thank your wife."

"They're, uh, from the lady whose dog I kept over the weekend. They were gone and it got loose when a pet sitter walked it."

Elizabeth grinned at him and turned to Skelly. "We're pretty sure how the syringe that killed him got to the hospital, and we think we know who administered the vodka. But we haven't figured out how the vodka got to the killer. Maybe at the same time as the syringe. We have more work to do."

"Anyone at the hospital involved?"

"I have no reason to think so."

Skelly laughed. "So, without even trying you made Philip Hargrove happy."

"The price I'll have to pay," Elizabeth said.

NEWS FROM THE SEARCH OF Milton Weeks' desk was not encouraging. The single-serving wine was there, sealed. He maintained that it was for use at home, because he paid attention to portion control. He kept the drawer locked so no one – especially any staff under twenty-one —could access the wine.

Mahan had called her from outside Weeks' office. "What else can we look for?"

"The warrant is only for the desk, right?"

"Yep."

Elizabeth closed her eyes in thought. "Does one of the drawers have folders with lots of papers?"

"Sure, just like Hammer's."

"Go through every piece, front and back. All we need is one receipt from the liquor store and we can link him to Yeltsin. If we can't prove he supplied the vodka, I hope we can back up Yeltsin about Weeks scrounging the syringes from him."

CALDERONE CALLED FROM THE hospital ten minutes later. "Franz and the mayor were in the cafeteria at the same time – they didn't arrive or leave together. But the camera doesn't show them at a table."

"They sat separately?"

"Don't know. There are two cameras. One shows the cash registers and a portion of the serving area behind them. Another the doors, which are near each other. That one picks up a few tables, but not all of them."

Elizabeth had been so sure they would see something. "Damn! I really wanted that connection."

"We did get something else," Calderone said. "You remember that Franz was on the second floor with those phony flowers? Well, real ones, for a phony purpose."

"I do. With her ball cap and bent head."

"The same day Dingle died, one of the housekeeping staff found a brand new bundle of flowers in a trash can in an unoccupied patient room. The rooms aren't locked, you know."

"What did said housekeeper do with them?"

"Unfortunately she threw them out. They aren't allowed to keep anything they find. But she knew a few of the kinds of flowers, and was certain of some of the colors. I think she'll be able to recognize it in a floral bouquet line-up."

"You practiced that, didn't you?" Elizabeth asked.

"You bet. But, also no Weeks on any security video. It would have been hard to avoid all the cameras."

Elizabeth sighed. "I feel like he's slipping away. I have to think of something."

MAYOR HUMPHREY NEVER called the police station. Elizabeth felt sure she knew Franz had been picked up, and that Milton Weeks' desk had been the subject of a search warrant.

From Maitlin, Hammer learned that Humphrey was scheduled to meet with Mrs. Washington about the nurse practitioner position. Watching from a distance, Mahan had confirmed Humphrey made the meeting, which was held at the community health center.

The mayor returned to her office and sat behind a closed door. Taylor learned this by stopping by City Hall with a report on his interactions with the three local schools. The mayor had previously said she'd like to see it, to use as a good example of positive community activities by city employees. Taylor spoke to

Heather Wilson, who said she'd give Humphrey the report when she finished eating a sandwich at her desk.

Elizabeth hoped the mayor was going bonkers, alone in her office.

At two-fifteen Mahan called. "I wish I could tell you different, Chief, but I can't find anything in that desk to link Weeks to the liquor store."

"How is he taking the search?"

"He's being ridiculously cheerful about it," Mahan said.

At two-thirty, Jerry Pew called with questions about Patricia Franz. Elizabeth wanted to ask him what took him so long.

"My contact in the state's attorney's office tells me she's being held as an accomplice to Dingle's murder! That nice lady."

"What did she do?" Elizabeth asked.

"Damn it, Chief. She wouldn't get to Donaldson without going through you."

"I can't tell you more than we interviewed her and Donaldson is considering charges."

"But they say she's an accomplice. That means more people."

"No dim bulbs in your brain, Jerry. I have to run." Elizabeth hung up.

ELIZABETH'S LAST HOPE LAY in about forty black bags of garbage retrieved from the dumpster behind City Hall. She had hired men who worked for the County Recycling Center to go through the bags Tuesday evening, supervised by Taylor. She would pay them from the police budget.

Thankfully, the bags did not have to come to the station. The manager said the men could use the drop-off area at the center. Trucks dumped their loads by early afternoon, and they had to be fully sorted each day. That left the very smelly swath of concrete uncluttered until the next morning.

Because the recycling staff started work early, their day ended at four and they could begin going through garbage bags at four-thirty. At six-thirty, Elizabeth took the workers a huge order of subs and cold bottles of soft drinks. The tallest, a man about thirty-five, who could best be described as shaggy, said, "You can hire us anytime."

"I hope I don't have to, but if I do, you'll be the first I call."

She and Taylor sat on a bench several yards from the center's entrance and watched the four men dive into the food. "You don't want any, Taylor?"

"I don't think I'll eat for a week."

She smiled. "Sorry you have to be here, but we can't risk them finding syringes or vodka bottles without one of us here."

"I don't mind, in my brain. It's my stomach that's mad about it."

Elizabeth sniffed the air. "It's a good thing this place is half-a-mile outside of town."

"Yeah. Before you moved here there were petitions to be sure the center wasn't near where people worked or lived."

"How many bags have they searched?"

"We've looked in all of them and picked out twelve to go through first. They seemed to have stuff from offices like the mayor's."

"And how did others look?"

"I guess the public information office cleaned house. Big bag of old files. The Transit Office has a bag of used bus transfers and passes, and somebody's really smelly banana peels. Lots of commentary from these guys about how much stuff was in the bag that should have been put in the recycling bins."

Elizabeth smiled. "I can imagine."

"Anyway, we'll go through all the bags, but I thought we'd start with the ones that seemed most likely."

The men tossed balled-up sandwich wrappers into a garbage can, yelled thanks, and walked toward the bags strewn across the floor of the recycling center.

Elizabeth acknowledged the thanks with a wave and turned to Taylor. "How late are you guys working?"

"Eight-thirty. They have to be back here at seven in the morning."

"Why don't you wait until noon tomorrow to come in?"

He grinned. "I should be out of the shower by then."

She winced. "Thanks aga…"

From the interior a voice yelled, "Taylor! We got an envelope with round things!"

Elizabeth and Taylor jogged into the recycling center. "Wait, let me open it," Taylor said. He pulled clean latex gloves from his pants pocket.

Elizabeth wanted to do the same, but decided this was essentially Taylor's collar. A short man with Italian features, wearing heavier gloves, passed Taylor a padded envelope about four by six inches. Elizabeth's heart quickened.

The envelope had been resealed loosely, and Taylor squeezed it lightly so he could look inside. He did, and grinned at Elizabeth. "Two plastic syringes."

Two of the men high-fived each other.

"Let's hope for fingerprints," Elizabeth said.

CHAPTER TWENTY

THE SIX-THIRTY AM PHONE call Wednesday morning rattled Elizabeth.

"Chief, it's Grayson. Bad news. Mayor Humphrey died from an overdose of hydrocodone mixed with alcohol."

"What?!"

"At two-twenty-three AM she sent an email to Heather Wilson's personal account telling her to send the police to her residence when Heather saw the email. Heather saw it at six-fifteen, and called 9-1-1.

"And county dispatch called you?"

"Yeah. I entered through the unlocked front door and found Humphrey's body in her bedroom, in bed. Pill bottle and empty liquor bottle on the bedside table."

Elizabeth met an ashen-faced Skelly and solemn Grayson at the mayor's residence a few minutes later. "How long has she been dead?"

Skelly shrugged. "My best guess now is within half-an-hour after she sent that email. I'll know more when I examine the contents of her stomach."

Grayson didn't seem able to take his eyes off the mayor as she lay motionless in her bed. "She looks so peaceful."

Final Operation

Elizabeth shook her head. "She must have realized we figured she had the most access to Dingle in the hospital. And a lot of reasons to want him out of her life."

"But why kill him right then?" Grayson asked. "She worked with him for years."

"She had the opportunity, I suppose," Skelly said.

"And partners." Elizabeth looked out the window of the mayor's bedroom to a yard blanketed in daffodils. She mentally went over the mayor's account of Dingle's last morning, as well as what Maitlin and Wilson had said. "I forget which admin staffer said Dingle had been in her desk without permission. That was part of their fight the morning he collapsed."

"Found something, you mean?" Grayson asked. "Like what?"

Skelly picked up the pill bottle with a gloved hand. "Maybe something like this. The name and prescription number have been scratched off."

"That makes no sense," Elizabeth said. "We'd have noticed if she took drugs regularly."

Grayson shrugged. "Maybe she didn't do it often. Just finding a bottle of opioid pills that weren't prescribed to her could have created a lot of pressure to resign."

"Dingle would have loved that," Elizabeth said. "Damn it all! We need to get Franz and Weeks."

"Taylor texted me that they found those syringes in an envelope just like the one in the cafeteria switch," Grayson said.

"No kidding," Skelly said. "Yesterday?"

"Evening," Elizabeth said. "They mostly implicate the mayor, since she did the handoff from Franz in the cafeteria. I…Damn. I wonder if she somehow heard we found them?"

"I'm not sure it would matter what she heard when," Skelly said. "If she knew she was going to get arrested at some point she might have seen suicide as preferable to shame and prison."

"Always a bad option." Elizabeth walked a couple steps closer and looked at Humphrey. She seemed to be sleeping. "A good lawyer could have painted her in a very sympathetic light. She might have served little time."

"What a waste," Grayson said.

NEWS OF THE MAYOR'S death rocketed through town. Elizabeth called Donaldson. "I don't want a second suicide."

"If you mean Franz, I agree. Anybody, of course. Fortunately, she has her son to consider."

"How old is he?" Elizabeth asked.

"Ten or eleven. He goes to the middle school."

"Will you send someone over to talk to her at county?" Elizabeth asked.

"Yes. She should be punished for passing what was essentially a weapon to a killer. But it'll be harder to justify a substantial sentence with the killer out of the picture."

"And it seems to have been Weeks who got the syringes from Yeltsin."

"His premeditation quotient is pretty high," Donaldson said. "Though we know about the syringes through that low-life Yeltsin."

"We'll get more. We have to."

Donaldson cleared his throat. "I'm going to offer a pretty fair deal to Franz's lawyer, Urich. If she pleads and gets most of her sentence suspended, maybe she'll spill on Weeks."

Calderone entered Elizabeth's office as she hung up. "I heard the last part of your call. Why do I feel like we're missing something?"

Elizabeth gestured to the chair across from her desk. "I keep thinking about our biggest break. If we hadn't gotten the phone call about looking in the wrong place and the screwy letter saying to look in the dumpster, we would never have staked it out, never have come across Franz looking for the syringes."

"And they came from Maitlin," Calderone said.

"She's admitted to the phone call about us looking in the wrong place. Hard to imagine two people were sending us advice."

"From the goodness of her heart," Calderone said. "Why not be direct?"

"If she's involved, she might not have wanted to be fingered for the tip." Elizabeth frowned. "So, she gets a medal or we have to wonder why she wanted to implicate her colleagues. Anonymously."

"Maybe she had a role," Calderone said. "Thought she could serve one or all of them on a platter and we wouldn't suspect her."

Elizabeth nodded, slowly. "You could be right. She'd know we couldn't place her in the hospital, but the mayor and Franz were there."

Calderone stood. "When do we get the fingerprints from the syringes Franz delivered to Humphrey?"

"I was going to ask you to lift them when you got in. See what you can match."

"If any match," Calderone said.

"Something will link our little band of killers. Does that liquor store have security cameras?" she asked.

"Not inside, I've looked."

Elizabeth thought for a minute. "Isn't it on the same street as Ramona's salon and the sub shop?"

"Yeah, but she's on a nicer block," Calderone said.

"She has a camera that points at the street. Maybe we can see Weeks driving by to go to the sub shop to meet Yeltsin."

"That's a long shot. I'll see who else in the area has one." He left.

Elizabeth called after him. "Do the fingerprint first, would you?"

CALDERONE CAME INTO ELIZABETH'S office half-an-hour later, as she was rereading notes of the interviews done to date.

"Processed the prints from the syringes," Calderone said.

"You also have a funny expression," Elizabeth said.

"You know how we do the prints for the background checks for city employees?"

"Sure. Whose prints?"

"Weeks and the Mayor's, like you'd expect. One unidentified index and part of a thumb, probably Dodd or his wife."

Elizabeth made a gimme gesture. "And…"

"Patricia Franz. That means she knew what was in that envelope she delivered to the mayor."

Elizabeth shook her head. "Donaldson will not be happy."

From the bullpen, Mahan said, "Yippee!"

Calderone and Elizabeth grinned at each other. "I love good news," she said.

Mahan said something to Hammer, who said, "Good one."

"Chief," Mahan called.

"Get in here and tell us."

Mahan grinned broadly as he walked in. "Didn't find any cameras in good spots to catch Weeks' car, but there was a different clerk in the sub shop when I called just now. He remembers seeing Weeks and Yeltsin together the morning Dingle was killed."

"Did he see Yeltsin give Weeks something?" Calderone asked.

"No, but when Yeltsin ordered a breakfast sub a few minutes later, he had a fifty dollar bill." Mahan laughed. "The guy who sold him the sandwich figured Yeltsin raided the cash drawer at the liquor store."

Elizabeth pointed her pen at Mahan. "Could have been what Weeks paid him for the syringes. Even if it's not, the fact that Weeks was seen with him bolsters what Yeltsin told us."

A VERY SMELLY SHOEBOX sat on Elizabeth's desk when she returned from lunch at the diner with a sulky Skelly. Sulky because he still hadn't been brought back to work.

"Hammer! Where did this damn box come from?"

He came to the doorway of her office. "The recycling guys brought it. Open it."

Elizabeth took a tissue from a box on her desk and lifted the lid. Inside was a mix of single-serving liquor bottles, most of them vodka. "These were from the City Hall bags?"

"From two bags, both from the suite where the mayor, Dingle, and Franz sit. Most of them were mixed in with the bits of paper from the shredder trash basket."

Elizabeth stared at the box, frustration mounting. "We didn't have anyone there when the guys found these. We should have kept looking last night. Or told them not to do more without Taylor."

"Suspects won't know that, and courts have said we're allowed to mislead a suspect."

"True. How does this great box play into it?" she asked.

"The recycling crew grabbed it from a bin of cardboard."

Elizabeth wrinkled her nose. "Then put the bottles in evidence bags and seal them. Stick the box in a separate one. I want to say bury it, but I suppose it's evidence."

Hammer grinned. "And get the Lysol."

Calderone and Taylor spent the afternoon lifting latent prints from the seventeen single-serve bottles. At three-forty-five, they came into Elizabeth's office with a list of names.

She read it. "Damn. Dingle didn't drink, but it looks like he drove everyone around him to imbibe."

Taylor laughed, and Calderone said, "Nearly all of the vodka bottles had Carolyn Maitlin's prints."

Elizabeth picked up her phone and called City Hall. She asked for Carolyn Maitlin and arched her eyebrows. "When was that? Thanks, Heather."

She hung up the phone and smiled at Calderone and Taylor. "Carolyn Maitlin's dear aunt just died. She's leaving town for a few days."

MAITLIN WAS BACKING OUT of the driveway of her neat bungalow when Elizabeth blocked her path with the Crown Vic. She got out and walked to Maitlin's car. Maitlin lowered the window.

"Afternoon, Ms. Maitlin."

Maitlin's puffy eyes and packed car told Elizabeth that most of what she thought she knew was true. "Sorry about your aunt. Looks like you're planning to stay a while."

"I appreciate your sympathy, Chief, but I have a long drive and want to get started."

Elizabeth smiled, pleasantly. "I need to check a couple of things first, starting with the town where your aunt died, and the name of the funeral home."

Maitlin put both hands on the steering wheel. She leaned forward until her head rested on it.

PATRICIAL FRANZ'S TONGUE LOOSENED when she heard Carolyn Maitlin was under suspicion for providing the vodka used to kill Donald Dingle.

With Urich urging she check every statement with him, Franz plowed on. "You have no idea what it was like. Maitlin was his little darling and the rest of us were his servants. More like indentured servants, but it would never end."

Elizabeth wanted to remind Franz that she could have changed jobs. She also recognized that Franz wouldn't know Humphrey was dead. She didn't plan to tell her until Franz had provided any details she could.

"What made the little darling turn against Dingle?"

"Dingle gave her a raise every year. But her salary was getting too high. He said he'd have to leave her at the same pay for a while. That didn't suit her at all. Didn't you ever wonder why she dressed so well?"

Franz seemed to want an answer. Elizabeth shook her head slowly. "I thought she always looked very put-together, but I don't pay a lot of attention to things like brands of clothing."

Franz's expression seemed to say Elizabeth should. "When Maitlin insisted she wanted that raise, Dingle started talking to her like he did the rest of us. The whole thing was her idea. She said if we all stuck together and kept our mouths shut, no one would ever know anything."

"Who is 'we?'" Elizabeth asked.

"The mayor, Milton Weeks, her, and me." Her tone grew bitter. "Too bad we didn't know how fast the vodka would kill him. We thought it would be harder to detect."

"And how did Weeks fit in?" Elizabeth asked.

"Maitlin called him. She had the vodka. Different kinds of little bottles hidden in places in the office. But she said vodka wouldn't smell as much."

Franz still hadn't mentioned Weeks' role. Elizabeth tried a different question to get to him. "Did she have the syringes, too?"

Franz shook her head. "We all knew Weeks drank a lot. She thought maybe he used, too, and would have syringes. She didn't want us to buy them anywhere that morning. I don't know where he got them."

"Where was Heather Wilson during all of this?" Elizabeth asked.

"She's always in her own world. You saw those earplugs she has. We talked in the mayor's office, mostly. Weeks made up some excuse to come up and fix her door. Pretty lame."

And yet, Elizabeth had initially believed him. She should have seen that for the ruse it was.

CHAPTER TWENTY-ONE

EN ROUTE TO THE STATION the next morning, Elizabeth stopped at Doris Minx's cookie shop and picked up two dozen donuts. One was for the guys at the station, the second for the crew at the recycling building. The smell of their workplace didn't seem to limit their appetites.

She stopped at the Recycling Center rather than ask one of her officers to do it. She left her jacket in the car so the smell wouldn't travel back to the station with her.

Elizabeth entered the station with the second box, and was surprised to find Wally Kermit in the chair next to Hammer's desk. "What brings you here?" Something about his expression said nothing good had done so.

Wally turned to her and, behind his back, Hammer gave Elizabeth a thumbs down gesture.

"Got myself fired from college security."

Elizabeth stopped a few feet from him. "Because you showed me that memo?"

Final Operation

"Yeah, I'm not sure how he figured it out. I thought I did a pretty good job when I said I found it the morning I brought it to his office."

Adrian Gangle's angry face came to Elizabeth. "Oh, no. I said something that let Adrian Gangle know I'd seen it. He must've known Dingle hadn't left a copy in his office at City Hall. That meant I had to have seen...You had to be the one to show me..."

Wally held up a hand, palm in Elizabeth's direction. "I was so damn mad about Dodd working with Dingle that I was going to start looking around."

Elizabeth placed the donuts on Hammer's desk. "I feel awful."

Wally shrugged. "I still got the chemistry teaching job. Til the end of the semester."

Still where Wally couldn't see him, Hammer pointed to his out box.

Elizabeth knew it held the vacancy announcement he'd been working on for her. The one she had hoped would help her create a more diverse force. "We have at least one opening in the next few weeks. I can't promise anything, but you can think about applying."

Wally grinned and turned to Hammer. "How about that?"

Elizabeth moved to stand in front of the doorway to the hall, so Wally didn't have to keep turning from her to Hammer.

"Hey, who's leaving?" Wally asked.

"No one, yet, but some people are close to retirement. We're such a small force I'm going to bring on a trainee so someone will be ready."

The phone rang and Hammer picked it up. He listened, then said, "Sure, I'll tell her." He hung up and looked at Elizabeth. "Skelly's back on the job."

Relief flooded through her. He wouldn't move. She'd still have Skelly. Now, what to do with him?

THE END

Books by Elaine L. Orr

If you don't find a book in your local bookstore, ask them to order a copy or check the library. All books are in paperback, ebook, large print, and often audio formats.

The Logland Series
Police procedurals with a cozy feel in small town Illinois
Tip a Hat to Murder
Final Cycle
Final Operation

The Jolie Gentil Cozy Mystery Series
The Jersey Shore can be fun with friends–except for the murders.
Appraisal for Murder
Rekindling Motives
When the Carny Comes to Town
Any Por t in a Storm
Trouble on the Doorstep
Behind the Walls
Vague Images
Ground to a Halt
Vague Images
Holidays in Ocean Alley
The Unexpected Resolution
The Twain Does Meet (novella)
Underground in Ocean Alley
Aunt Madge and the Civil Election (long short story)
Sticky Fingered Books
New Lease on Death

The Rivers Edge Series
Iowa nice meets murder along the Des Moines River.

The Family History Mystery Series
Truths of old to solve crimes today in the Maryland Mountains.

About Elaine L. Orr

Elaine L. Orr writes four mystery series: the Jolie Gentil series at the Jersey shore, the River's Edge series along Iowa's Des Moines River, the Logland series in small-town Illinois, and the Family History Mystery series in the Western Maryland Mountains.

What makes Elaine's fiction different from other traditional mysteries is the dry humor and the empathy her characters show to others. Fiction can't 'lecture' readers. But it can contain people whose paths we cross every day — whether we know it or not.

Elaine also writes plays and novellas, including her favorite, *Falling Into Place*. *Behind the Walls* was a 2014 Chanticleer Mystery and Mayhem Award shortlister, and *Demise of a Devious Neighbor* was shortlisted in 2017. *The Unscheduled Murder Trip* received an Indie BRAG Medallion in 2021. Elaine is a member of Sisters in Crime and the International Book Publishers Association.

http://www.elaineorr.com
http://www.elaineorr.blogspot.com
https://www.instagram.com/elaine.orr1/

Printed in the USA
CPSIA information can be obtained
at www.ICGtesting.com
LVHW021346051023
760085LV00064B/1927